I0603531

NONSENSE IN THE NORTH

SAILING, SMUGGLING, SPYING AND AVOIDING SHARKS, SNAKES AND SPIDERS

JANE ELLYSON

Copyright © Jane Ellyson 2021

The moral right of the author has been asserted.

All rights reserved. No part of this publication may be reproduced or transmitted by any person or entity (including Google, Amazon or similar organisations), in any form or by any means electronic or mechanical, including photocopying, recording, scanning or by any information storage and retrieval system or transmitted in any form, or by any means without the prior written permission of the publisher.

This novel is a work of fiction. Names and characters are the product of the author's imagination and any resemblance to actual persons, living or dead is entirely coincidental.

A catalogue record for this book is available from the National Library of Australia.

ISBN: 978-0-6451358-2-4 (PBK)
ISBN: 978-0-6451358-3-1 (e-book)

Editor: Jackie Bates
Cover Design by nabinkarna on Fiverr
Map by scrollavezza

www.janeellyson.com

❀ Created with Vellum

PRAISE FOR NONSENSE IN THE NORTH

Scott's missing.
As a former intelligence officer, Charlotte needs to use all her
skills to find him, to capture El Tigre and to shut his network
down.

Nonsense in the North delivers a trifecta of joy. It's a thriller as
Charlotte seeks to find an international drug cartel, travels
through inhospitable bushland while searching for Scott, all the
while supporting her best friend's wedding preparations.

Can Charlotte find Scott, bust open a drug cartel and get her
bridesmaid's dress, before she walks down the aisle at her best
friend's wedding?

Finding someone in the Australian bush is akin to finding a needle in a haystack. With the clock ticking, Charlotte follows a softly spoken Aboriginal tracker named Nev across Cape Conway National Park, avoiding stinging trees, poisonous snakes and cunning estuarine crocodiles.

FAMILY TREE

BOURNES, HARMONS, WYATTS

Ellen (deceased) m. George Bourne m. Helen Harmon

Melissa m. Andrew Wyatt   Louis m Jenny

Scott (deceased)   Charlotte   Scott   Miranda

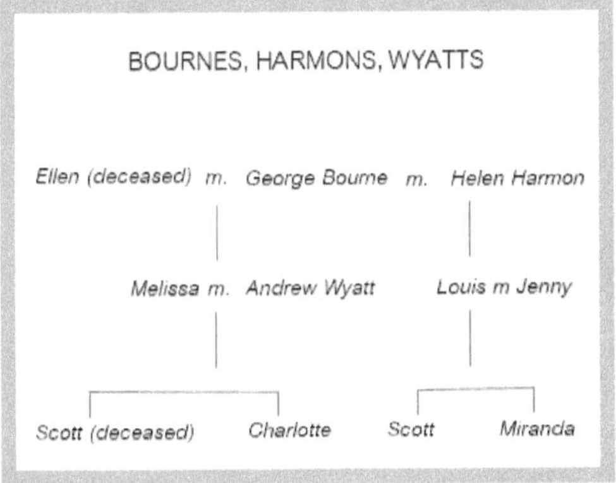

MAP OF NORTH QUEENSLAND, AUSTRALIA

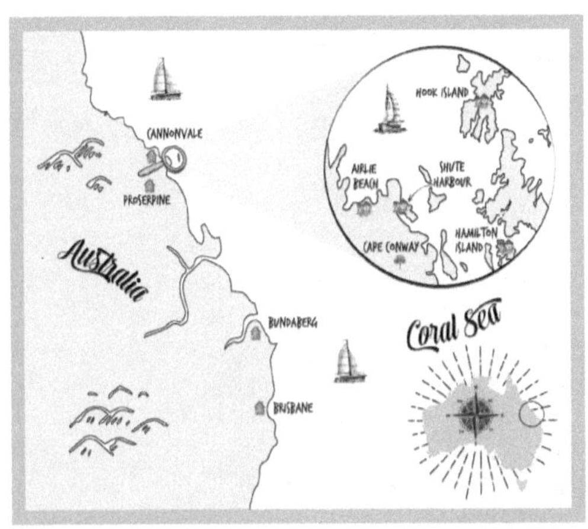

PROLOGUE

Mon 8 Feb 8:oopm

Sharks were circling the yacht. Scott thought this amusing as there were also sharks aboard. Humour was his go-to-strategy when under pressure. How had he not seen trouble coming? Looking back on the past week and thinking about his conversations with Pedro Gatos, the signs were there and he'd missed them all. Potentially explaining his involvement with *The Tiger's* drug cartel to the police was the least of his worries. Making sure he made it back to shore with all his limbs in place was a bigger concern.

1

___

CHARLOTTE: SAT 6 FEB

Charlotte was awoken by the sound of the window shade in the row in front being opened by the flight attendant. She'd fallen asleep three hours earlier, midway through watching Titanic, and her interrupted dream had been directly influenced by the last scene she'd watched. Sleep had overcome her just as Leonardo Di Caprio had wrapped his arms around Kate Winslet on the bow of the ship. She could still feel Scott Harmon's arms around her, as he whispered in her ear about the wonderful future they were headed for. Remembering how the movie ended, she was rather pleased at the point at which sleep had overcome her. The past ten days had been at times a near disaster, and she didn't need to be reminded of this. She'd completed her first and last assignment as an occasional intelligence officer for the Australian Security and Intelligence organisation (ASIO) and was looking forward to this new phase in her life, with a focus on having a fabulous time with Scott.

Charlotte looked across the row to her best friend (and

Scott's sister), Miranda Harmon, who was still sound asleep, gently snoring with her blond bobbed head resting on the shoulder of her fiancé, Mason Murray. Mason pushed his glasses up his nose and crinkled a smile at Charlotte. The rattle of the trolleys bearing warm drinks and forgettable omelettes, started its journey down the aisle. Miranda woke with a start, noisily yawned and rubbed her neck.

'How long till we land?' she asked Charlotte.

'Two hours until we touch down again on Australian soil. I hope you've had a good sleep; you're going to be busy.'

'I know and I'm so excited. Getting married, moving to England and oh gosh, all the things that'll come after that. You will come and visit us, won't you C?'

'Of course. But not immediately. I suspect that you two love birds will want to spend a bit of time alone. And also because I need to focus on getting Chic Charlie going.'

'But you could do a business trip and get a tax deduction by coming to buy fabrics, say from Liberty's of London?'

'Yes, indeed I could. But I want to find local fabric providers first. And believe me, you'll be busy. You'll have fun and won't have time to be lonely in London, particularly with Mason there.'

'But I'm not as adventurous as you, C.'

'And that's a good thing, M. Stop worrying. I will come. And who knows, I may even bring your brother with me.'

'And we could all go off on holiday somewhere in Europe? Say Monte Carlo or Rome or Taormina? These are all places you know well, aren't they? Or we could go sailing?'

Charlotte bit her lip and for a moment was lost in her

memories. There were experiences in each of those places that she was not interested in repeating. She'd been kidnapped, stalked and compromised. It was better to go somewhere new.

'Coffee or tea?' the crisply dressed attendant asked, interrupting her thoughts.

'Tea please. Thank you. How long till we land?'

'About ninety minutes. Looking forward to being home?'

'Always,' Charlotte replied with emphasis.

Six pink balloons floated above the fray, printed with the words *She Said Yes*, making it easy to spot Miranda and Mason's parents in the Arrivals hall at Brisbane International. The balloons weren't necessary as location markers in the busy airport as the familial collective could also be heard shrieking, *They're here!* as the trio emerged from Customs. The communal delight was both embarrassing and intoxicating for Miranda and Mason. For a moment, Charlotte, didn't see her own parents standing at the back of the hall as she greeted the Murrays and Harmons. They were enjoying watching the joyful reunion. Charlotte sauntered over and gave them both a hug.

'Welcome home, honey,' her dad said, ruffling her hair.

'Thanks for coming to get me.'

'Of course. Now it's probably going to be a bit hectic these coming weeks, helping Miranda get ready for the wedding. Quite a change from being on retreat. Hope you had a good rest. You're going to be busy.'

Charlotte smiled. 'Ready to go. Just let me say goodbye

to the others.' She walked back to Miranda and Mason's family gathering.

'We're heading off now. See you all in a couple of days.' Miranda gave her the phone hand signal and mouthed *call every day*. Charlotte gave her the thumbs up and waved goodbye.

On the drive back to their home at Kangaroo Point, while her parents briefed her on events of *great importance* that had occurred during her absence, she scrolled her messages.

Message from Scott. *What a race! Well it wasn't really a race. Just a trial in preparation for the real thing later on this year. We survived squalls, breaching whales and tsunami waves. And I've just been offered a one-day gig from Hamilton Island. I've booked us into the Reef View Hotel and left instructions for there to be a key for you at reception. Have a think about where you'd like to go for dinner, or perhaps you'd prefer room service? There's a breathtaking view from the balcony and inside is rather lovely too.* 🛎

Message from Charlotte. *Sounds wonderful. Super excited. Flight to be booked today. Will be v. busy 4 next 24 hrs supporting your sister with decisions to get this wedding rocking in 2 weeks. BTW the colour theme for the wedding is silver. So U and Mason need silver ties + vests & I need slinky silver gown. Looking forward to seeing you.*

Message from Scott. *Looking forward to seeing that slinky silver gown.*

2

THE TIGER: PORT VILA, VANUATU SAT 30 JAN

The tiny rodent in the mousetrap glared, unblinking at El Tigre (The Tiger). The simple contraption had caught it across the back rather than breaking his neck. The latter action would have killed him instantly. He was now slowly suffering and wondering what the beast hovering above him would do next. The man's lips curled in a cruel smile before he gently rested his boot on the mouse's head, ignoring his squeals for mercy, pushing ever so gently until the rodent's brains catapulted out of his mouth.

The man wiped his foot on a towel and called for the deck hand to remove the carcass and clean up the mess. He sat down at the table where his laptop was open on a yachting Facebook page. He stared at the member's profile. While he'd never met him or spoken with him, and he was highly motivated to keep a level of separation from people participating in his business, he wanted to meet this yacht captain. The trial yacht race from Port Vila to Bundaberg was a perfect opportunity to observe the man firsthand and to assess his yachting skills as well as his capacity for undertaking a more significant role in his operations. First, he needed to establish if he could trust him.

Pedro Gatos firmly shook Scott Harmon's hand as they met for the first time at the Waterfront Bar and Grill.

'Fantastic sunset, eh?' Scott observed.

'Indeed it is,' Gatos replied. 'And hopefully we will see many more like this on the trip to Bundaberg.'

'Looking forward to it,' Scott replied.

'You do know that this isn't the best time for sailing? We're likely to encounter wild, cyclonic storms.'

'I'm up for it. And the anticipation of stormy waters ahead is reflected in the price you're paying for my services.'

'That's the spirit, boy. I believe in reward relative to risk. Looking forward to getting to know you better on this trip, Scott.'

'Likewise, Pedro.'

After dinner they inspected the yacht, discussed the seven-day weather forecast and reviewed the planned route. Pedro listened carefully. Scott demonstrated detailed nautical knowledge and it would be interesting to see how this knowledge was applied in practise. As Scott waved goodbye from the ramp and headed back to his hotel, Pedro lit up a cigar and inhaled deeply. Juan Gomez, his number two, joined him on the bridge. Juan towered over Pedro by two heads. He was lanky, heavily tattooed and weather worn, not just from having spent a lifetime on the sea but from having been addicted to the products he now distributed. His deep loyalty to Pedro

Gatos, the drug king more frequently referred to as El Tigre, stemmed from Pedro's assistance in helping him break his addiction to cocaine. The brain damage he'd sustained from his addiction meant that the irony of his situation was lost on him.

'So?' Juan asked.

'Don't know,' Pedro replied. 'We'll see.'

Large swells were building when they pushed off from Port Vila the following morning. Scott demonstrated his sailing prowess by ploughing through the two-metre waves, buffeting the twenty-three-metre cutter.

They routed north of New Caledonia and Chesterfield Reef to skirt Bampton Reef before turning southwest to Bundaberg. A high-pressure system coming up from Tasmania provided two days of sailing with steady wind, albeit with heavy accompanying squalls. Scott was able to manoeuvre the vessel quickly away from an unexpected coral shelf near the Chesterfield reef, earning the admiration of his sailing companions. It was dangerous sailing past Bampton Reef with frequently changing wind direction. Several sharks swam by close to the surface, eyeing the vessel with interest.

On day four they watched in awe as a pod of breeching humpback whales surfaced nearby and then received radio notification of an earthquake measuring at 6.3 on the Richter scale, ninety kilometres north of Vanuatu in the Shefa province. Two minutes later a tsunami warning was issued on the radio and seagulls flew overhead, noisily sounding their own cautionary message. The three men raced to secure the vessel and attach their harnesses. Ten minutes later, several waves of four metres in height, and hundreds of kilometres long, gently lifted and then dropped *Latin Libertad*. The descent was more problematic than the rise but the yacht, and all aboard her, kept their balance. An hour later they celebrated with apple cider and cashew nuts. They dared not drink champagne in case aftershocks meant they needed to repeat the process.

Seven days later they sailed into perfect weather conditions with a clear sky and winds at ten to fifteen knots. Scott radioed ahead to Australian customs, letting them know the expected time of arrival into Bundaberg. Shortly afterwards a customs plane flew over and was carefully observed by Pedro and Juan. They sailed into Bundaberg around 11:00am the following morning. Quarantine inspectors were rigorous in checking the yacht's obvious and less obvious crevices, removing bananas from the fridge and rice from the lock-up. They joked amiably with Scott as they undertook their duties, and commended him on sailing across the ocean at this time of year and asking how they manoeuvred the craft during the tsunami. There was a liberal dollop of drama in the retelling of the story, which everyone enjoyed.

Pedro was delighted with Scott's performance and asked him if he was interested in another yachting contract, this one of a short-term nature, departing from Hamilton Island. Scott couldn't believe his luck and accepted immediately. As he ran down the gang plank with his bag, Pedro lit another cigar and turned to Juan.

'He's not our money man. I've just received an email from The Squirrel recommending a different process for the next transfer. But you have to agree he's a remarkable sailor, and more importantly, has established a good relationship with customs authorities. We'll use him for this next trip where we *collect fish* while we're sailing, and if he gives us any trouble, he can go swimming somewhere a long way from shore. I'll send a message to The Squirrel telling him to rendezvous with us at Airlie Beach. Secure the *Latin Libertad*. She'll be resting here a while.'

THE SQUIRREL: SYDNEY SAT 30 JAN

The Squirrel smiled. The invitation to fly to Hamilton Island represented a significant shift in his relationship with The Tiger. He was impressed by the professional operation of the syndicate and the protocols in place to keep communications secure. At all times he was to use his moniker of *The Squirrel* and not his name. The goods being purchased through the business were referred to as *fish*, and any transfer process as *the market* while funds were called *bait*. He'd originally been approached because of the small money-remitting services he provided, enabling individuals and companies to sends funds overseas for a fee. The first few transactions had been small, clearly to test the service. But lately they'd been increasing in frequency and size and he'd sent a message to The Tiger proposing alternate channels to avoid the attention of the regulatory authorities, who were always on the lookout for potential money laundering. This communication had prompted the invitation to fly to Hamilton Island for a face-to-face meeting, ostensibly to advise on the purchase of a barramundi fish farm for the business. His flights and accommodation had been paid for in advance and he'd already identified a suitable property.

SCOTT: MON 8 FEB 6:00AM

The *Ojo Del Tigre* was a larger yacht than the *Latin Libertad*. It was a thirty-five metre motor-powered Sunseeker and was clearly very new. Registered in the Cayman Islands to a company no one locally seemed to have heard of, it stood out amongst the other yachts, sitting nobly at the marina. Scott called out 'Ahoy!' as he walked across the gang plank, attracting the attention of a weathered looking man wearing an apron, who emerged from the galley.

'I'm Scott. Captain Scott today,' he announced.

'They're on the bridge, matey,' the chef replied in a distinctly disrespectful tone. Pedro and Juan stopped talking as Scott walked up the stairs and onto the bridge. The silence was surprising, but quickly broken by Pedro.

'Morning Scott. Did you meet Fred?'

'Indeed I did.'

'Don't be put off by his manners. He's been recruited for his cooking and not his interpersonal skills.'

'No worries Pedro. I'm used to accommodating different temperaments on the yachts I've captained.'

'Estupendo. Let's go fishing!'

Several hours later, Pedro signalled for Scott to anchor near a coral reef, where birds were diving en masse into the water, a clear sign that tuna were below. The three men cast their lines and over the next hour pulled in a number of tuna and trevally. Fred grilled the fish and Scott had to admit that the grumpy one, as he referred to him in his head, was a good chef. They moved locations after lunch and changed lures in the hope of snagging game-fish. While they sat and waited Pedro smoked his cigar. Suddenly Scott's rod bent dramatically and he stood up in his seat to brace. At the same time another boat approached from the north.

'Vegetables are here Fred. Juan, can you help him while I give Scott a hand with this beauty.' Scott heard Fred greet the fisherman on the other boat in Bahasa, before taking delivery of several boxes of mangoes and coconuts.

That's odd, Scott thought, before being distracted by the mighty marlin fighting him on the line. Mangoes and coconuts were both easily available on shore. Maybe Fred hadn't had time to go shopping before they left? Scott rolled then released the marlin, managing to bring the beautiful black beast close to the boat, before time was called and it was given its freedom. Pedro slapped him on the back and offered him a beer. He refused. 'I've been paid to get you all back to shore safely. I'll be happy to join you for a drink then.'

'I respect that Scott, and I'm very impressed by the way you managed that marlin. How're your arms feeling?'

'Fine. They might be a little stiff in a couple of hours though.'

'You look like you lift weights. Is that what you do to keep so fit?'

'No. I surf and hike whenever I can, and I find that working on a yacht is pretty physical.'

'Indeed it is. Particularly when you're working for me.'

'Should we head back to the marina now?' Scott asked, trying to disguise how excited he was at the prospect of seeing Charlotte again.

'No, it's going to be a late night. Best fishing is at night on a rising tide. We're going to move position. Enjoy another feast cooked up by little Freddy, and then we'll see.'

Scott nodded but felt a moment of disquiet. Charlotte would be wondering where he was and he had no way to contact her, having lost mobile phone service shortly after they left Hamilton Island that morning. He returned to the bridge and moved the yacht to the new fishing position, further down the reef. As he leaned over to check the location of the anchor, several tiger sharks swam past.

'They're also fishing,' Pedro said watching him while he lit another cigar. 'It's not a good time to go swimming, I think.'

'Agree. No one would even find your bones if these guys got a hold of you.'

'Scott, I understand you've been on yachts all round the world, met all sorts of people. I imagine been in a few interesting situations.'

'Yeah, sure have,' Scott replied.

'What's the worst thing you've ever done while you've been at sea and not told your parents?' Scott was a little alarmed by the question but disguised his reaction by raising his right eyebrow, lifting his chin and stroking his goatee.

He remembered the time that he and Charlotte were taken prisoner on Ille Sainte Marguerite in France by a particularly nasty mobster. They'd escaped with the help of Royal Marines and had vowed to keep this misadventure a secret for the benefit of many, not least of which were Charlotte's parents. Not too long after this he'd borrowed the yacht he was captaining to rescue four women sold into slavery off the coast of Sicily. The story made the European press because a journalist who just happened to be his best friend, was on the pier in Messina when all the yachts came in. His involvement in the breakup of this international crime syndicate was now well known and he was happy with that. Scott looked at Pedro.

'Well, I've been away from Australia for extended periods and I'm not that good at communicating. I guess that's caused my parents anxiety. They worry that I could go missing and they wouldn't know where I was.'

'And that's it?' Gatos asked.

'Well. That's all I'm prepared to fess up to,' he said with a cheeky grin. The Tiger smiled and slapped him on the back.

'Good for you, lad. Yes, we all need to keep our secrets safe.' Pedro took a deep drag on his cigar and regarded Scott thoughtfully again. 'So what are your dreams?'

'I'd like to own a yacht like this and sail around the world.' A scream from the galley interrupted the conversation and they both raced downstairs to discover that Fred had inadvertently sliced open his hand. Scott went to the first aid kit, retrieving disinfectant and bandages.

'Sit down, Fred. Juan, can you check the stove and mop up this blood,' he ordered slipping back into captain command mode. He looked at Fred's wound. 'This needs stitches if it's to heal properly. There. That's the best I can do for now. Sit there and keep your hand elevated and still. I'll get dinner.' Scott signalled to Juan to lay out four plates. He turned to the stove and could see that the meal was nearly ready. Fred had been cooking grilled fish with coconut rice. He'd cut himself while preparing a side dish of mango salsa. Scott threw the bloody pulp in the bin and went to the larder to pull another mango from the food box that had been delivered earlier. As he pulled the fruit from the box, he noticed a large plastic package containing a white substance. He knew instantly that it was cocaine and that he was now in serious trouble. Turning slowly, he reached for the now clean knife, and started carving the mango. Both Pedro and Juan had seen him look at the cocaine. Before anyone could speak, he cleared his throat and made an announcement, 'I'll serve up now, and we can then discuss how this special fruit will be delivered over dinner.'

Pedro regarded him carefully. 'Welcome to the tiger's lair, Scott.'

CHARLOTTE: MON 8 FEB 11:00AM

Charlotte was seated beside a couple who'd got married that morning and were flying to Hamilton Island for their honeymoon. They spent the trip reliving every moment of their special day. Someone in the bridal party was an aspiring professional photographer and had taken more than 1,000 photos. Charlotte sensed that the groom was becoming a little bored at image 629. There was an exchange of pleasantries as sandwiches were served and Charlotte was shown the website where the best of the wedding and honeymoon photos would be shared. She also discovered that Rachel and Brad would be staying at the same hotel. There were polite farewells offered at the luggage carousel with vague suggestions made about the four of them catching up for a drink. These offers were made in the full knowledge that it was unlikely to happen. Charlotte collected the key from reception and let herself into the hotel room. There was a note on the hotel stationery from Scott, saying he'd be back by 4:00pm. Her phone rang.

'Hi Mrs Murray,' Charlotte said.

'Oh, I love the sound of that,' Miranda cooed.

'How's the planning going?'

'Brilliantly. Got a venue at Kangaroo Point, right beside Brisbane River as a result of a late cancellation. Apparently, the groom-to-be was caught *in flagrante delicto* with one of the *bridesmaids-no-more*. Was also able to scoop up their wedding celebrant. Double bonus. So I need you and my brother back in Brissie for the big day on the 20th. Capichi?'

'You bet. In the diary. Have you decided which website to host your wedding photos on?'

'No – thank you for thinking of that. Will add that to the list of jobs to be done,' Miranda said,

'Speaking of jobs, I need to visit a couple of boutiques before your brother's boat comes in. Let me know once you've got your frock.'

'Of course,' Miranda replied.

'Happy planning. Talk soon.'

There was a boutique and a gift store in the hotel lobby. Charlotte spoke to the owner of the boutique, who wasn't interested in taking on new suppliers at this time, but was happy to take her card. Charlotte then called into the gift store, which sold art works and small gifts, designed to be purchased as holiday mementoes. She was drawn to several Aboriginal paintings, images from which had been used for t-shirts, sarongs and as a cover for small notebooks. It was difficult to choose between the designs, but she finally made a selection and took her purchases to the front counter.

'Gifts or for yourself?'

'Bit of both. I'd love to know who the artist is. I love these designs.'

'You're speaking to them. Hi, I'm Yindi.' Yindi and Charlotte spent ten minutes sharing their mutual love of design and fabric, with Charlotte concluding the discussions by ordering several rolls of fabric that would be converted into corporate work wear. She took her purchases back to the hotel room and sat on the bed. She hated waiting. She glanced at her phone again. One minute had passed since she'd last looked. It was 4:11pm. She knew it was perfectly normal for Scott to have been delayed on his return trip. Change of wind conditions was the most likely reason, but he could of course have stopped to rescue someone. She called his phone, which immediately went through to voicemail.

Message for Scott. *4:12pm Hey sailor. I've safely arrived on Hamilton Island. Am coming down to the marina to greet you. Call me as soon as you can so we don't miss each other.*

Message for Scott. *4:30 Lovely here at the marina. Found a great spot for dinner. Call me. Soon.*

As Charlotte paced the marina, she noticed a police vessel. She called out for permission to come aboard and a young Aboriginal policewoman came out on deck.

'Hello. Can I help?'

'My boyfriend is missing.'

'How long since you've last seen him?'

'Two weeks, cause I've only just returned to Australia from Thailand.'

'You were in Thailand, eh?'

'Well, only briefly.'

'Where do you believe your boyfriend to be?'

'On a yacht he was captaining.'

'And the name of the yacht?'

'Oh. I'm not sure. Something Spanish? Scott only recently arrived back himself from Vanuatu and was supposed to be doing a one-day cruise. He's not back yet, and he's not answering his phone.' The officer asked her name and Charlotte told her.

'Take a seat and I'll make a few enquiries. I'm Sergeant Sillago, you can call me Kirra.' Charlotte sat down and looked at her phone while the sergeant tapped on the computer. A few minutes later another officer joined them in the small cabin. He offered her a drink and opened his laptop.

'Can we ask you a few questions?'

'Of course,' Charlotte replied anxiously.

'What was the purpose of your trip to Thailand?'

'What?'

'Your recent trip to Thailand. What was the purpose?'

'Holiday. I was there with friends,' she said.

'Where'd you go?'

'Krabi, Mae Sot, Bangkok. Look, I don't see what that has to do with Scott.'

'Was he with you in Thailand?'

'Yes. For some of the time. He left early to fly to Vanuatu.'

'And why did he go to Vanuatu?'

'Because he got a sailing gig to Bundaberg. They were practicing for a race.'

'And who was this gig with?'

'I didn't pay too much attention to be honest. Some international crowd. From South America I think.'

'Did he know that it's not advised to sail across the ocean at this time of year because of the potential for cyclones?'

'I guess that they wanted to test his skills.'

'I see. Can we have more details about Scott?' Charlotte provided his full name and date of birth. She could see the police officer's eyebrows flicker ever so briefly once she provided this information. 'Wait here please.' The two officers went up onto the deck to chat privately. Something was wrong. They were asking her surprising questions. She didn't expect questions about Thailand, and she was certainly not open to disclosing how she'd spent her time while she was there and also in Myanmar. They didn't need to know that she was an occasional intelligence officer for the Australian Security Intelligence Organisation, well, that she used to be. That career was now over. The questions about Thailand made her think they suspected she was involved in trafficking drugs.

Charlotte jumped as her phone rang. Maybe it was Scott. She inwardly groaned when she saw that it was Miranda.

'Hi M,' she said with a lightness in her voice that she didn't feel. She listened and agreed as Miranda talked about offering drinks and nibbles for guests while the wedding photos were being taken. The police officer smiled when she rang off.

'You've got wedding responsibilities?'

'Yes. And getting the bride's brother back for the wedding is pretty important. Can you help me?'

'It's difficult when you're not one hundred percent certain he's missing and you don't know the name of the vessel he was on. Give us your number and go back to your hotel. I'll call you if I receive any information I can share with you.'

'What do you mean, if you can share with me? What is it you're not telling me?'

'I'm sorry, Charlotte. I can't tell you. There's an ongoing investigation and my hands are tied. Come back tomorrow when I may be able to tell you more.'

SCOTT: MON 8 FEB 8:00PM

Sharks were circling the yacht. Scott thought this amusing as there were also sharks aboard. Humour was his go-to-strategy when he was under pressure. He chastised himself. How had he not seen trouble coming? Looking back on the past week and thinking about his various conversations with Pedro Gatos since they'd left Port Vial in Vanuatu, the signs were there – and he'd missed them all. Explaining his involvement with The Tiger's drug cartel to the police was the least of his worries. Making sure he made it back to shore with all his limbs in place was a bigger concern. Scott knew his choices were limited. A plan was building in his head as he took his seat at the dining room table beside Pedro. Juan carried the plates out and took the seat besides Fred, who was subdued. Scott knew that with Fred's injury, they were even more likely to need him to transport the drugs.

'Eat,' Pedro instructed picking up his knife and fork. There was an uneasy silence as they collectively cut the grilled fish.

'This is delicious, Fred,' Scott offered, as he took a

second bite. It was a surreal moment and one he knew he would remember for a long time. Fred barely acknowledged the compliment.

'You'll need to take the fish to the designated market.' Scott was confused and looked from Pedro to Juan. 'There's a lot of fish, as you know, and you'll need to carry them for several kilometres in specially designed backpacks. For this trip you'll need to wait for additional bait before collecting the delivery van and meeting me at Airlie Beach.'

'I'll do whatever Juan says,' Scott replied. Pedro nodded.

'You'll need to give me your phone. There's no mobile coverage anywhere near the market, and leaving it inactive with me limits the opportunity for anyone to find you.' Scott was reluctant to comply but knew he had no choice. He pulled the phone from his pocket and pushed it across the table. Pedro picked it up and looked at the image of Charlotte that Scott used as his screen saver.

'Goodness, she's lovely.' Scott froze. 'Don't worry lad. I'll return it to you when we celebrate your successful transaction at Fish D'vine and The Rum Bar at Airlie Beach. You'll also receive the first down payment for your yacht.' Scott glared at Pedro and nodded ever so slightly. It was not accidental that The Tiger had commented on his girlfriend's beauty. This was a threat to her, as well as his life.

7

CHARLOTTE: MON 8 FEB 8:00PM

Charlotte returned to the hotel. She waved to Yindi. Brad and Rachel, the honeymooners from her flight, were in the shop, and thought she was waving at them. They rushed out to greet her and show her the t-shirts and sarongs they'd just purchased.

'Which do you prefer?' Rachel asked, shoving two designs in front of her.

'That's like asking me to choose between cheesecake and key lime pie,' Charlotte replied. 'They're both beautiful.'

'Here, put this on,' Rachel insisted, thrusting a t-shirt at her. 'Brad. Take a photo of us.'

'I think we should also get the artist in the picture.'

'Who?' Rachel asked, confused.

'Yindi. The woman who served you.' Charlotte leaned behind Brad's back to wave at Yindi and to invite her to join them. Several photos were taken by and with Yindi, and promises were again made for the two couples to catch up once Scott had returned.

Charlotte held a whisper of hope that Scott would be

in their room as she opened the door. There were scraping noises on the balcony and she rushed outside to discover a flock of sulphur crested cockatoos making themselves at home. She was surprised none of the cheeky creatures flew away as she took a seat on the balcony. Indeed, several flew to the small table that she was sitting at and regarded her carefully.

'Hello there,' Charlotte offered. 'Don't s'pose you've seen a rather attractive bloke, who's this high with a gorgeous grin, and ...' The ping on her phone stopped her chat with the newly acquired feathered friends. It was a message from Miranda.

- *Florist* ✓
- *Photographer* ✓
- *Invitations sent* ✓

Charlotte texted back.

Bravo bride-to-be 👏

Seconds later Charlotte's phone rang, making her jump. It was Mason.

'Hey Mason. What's up?'

'Is Scott with you?'

'No. Not at the moment.'

'Please berate him for his poor telephone manners when you see him.'

'I intend to,' Charlotte replied curtly. 'How's everything in Brissie?'

'Miranda is doing all the heavy lifting for the wedding and it appears to be coming together. I'm trying desperately to find an interesting fashion story for *Hello* so I don't lose my job. Any ideas?'

'Well. I've discovered a wonderful Aboriginal artist here whose designs are available in fabric. She's made a few pieces in resort wear and I think there's opportunity for corporate wear too. Well, that's my plan. I'll send you a photo and you can decide. And by the way, Hamilton Island is a lovely location for a photo shoot.'

'Intriguing. I'll look at the snap, chat to Jane at *Hello* and let you know. You may well have a visitor. Hope you two won't mind the interruption to your break?'

Charlotte said nothing and wondered if she should share her concerns. Mason noticed the silence. 'You OK? Are you managing to keep out of trouble, Miss Wyatt?'

'As always,' she replied before saying goodbye and hanging up. She may have been keeping out of trouble but she was fairly sure that Scott was in the thick of something nefarious. She thought about her conversation with the police officer. Charlotte was worried Sergeant Sillago wouldn't be able to tell her anything about what was going on. What if she couldn't even tell her the name of the boat? Remembering that Teal had been in Vanuatu, she rang her office at the Australian Embassy in Paris.

Teal Dubois' official job title was Director of International Treaties. She also worked for the Australian Securities Intelligence Organisation (ASIO) in a role that wasn't entirely clear to Charlotte. She'd met Teal at a party on a yacht in Rome, just before she got caught up in an international slavery ring. Teal had provided surprising support and then invited her to accept a more formal association with ASIO, resulting in an intelligence gathering trip to Myanmar, just as the generals staged a military coup. There'd been a disagreement about the way her first assignment had been concluded, but Charlotte was confident Teal would put bygones aside and help her. The phone went directly to voicemail.

'Teal. It's Charlotte Wyatt. I urgently need information about a yacht that left Port Vila in Vanuatu ten days ago. It sailed to Bundaberg with Scott Harmon as captain. Who owns this yacht and who else was on it? I also need to know who owns the yacht that left Hamilton Island yesterday, again skippered by Scott Harmon, destination unknown. I don't know the name of either vessel, although I think they're Spanish.' Charlotte walked back into the room to retrieve her notebook and pen and started scribbling down questions. Five minutes later her phone pinged.

> **Message from Teal.** *Latin Libertad and Ojo del Tigre are owned by Panamanian Pedro Gatos. He's under international surveillance for drug trafficking and a major swoop is expected shortly. Warning. Keep away from Gatos, (he's very nasty) and the operation. PLEASE.*

The PLEASE in capital letters made Charlotte smile. The main reason she was no longer an intelligence officer for the Australian government was her intransigence. Charlotte walked back out onto the balcony. It was a magnificent view, but she took no joy in it knowing that Scott was somewhere out at sea, and most likely in grave danger.

8

SCOTT: TUE 9 FEB 1:00AM

Scott pulled up the anchor, turned the yacht around and headed back across the Coral Sea. He ran the plan, as it had been explained to him, over in his mind in a bid to identify an escape opportunity. He hadn't been told yet where or when they would land or *go to market* –the coded language they used to talk about the exchange of drugs for money. There'd clearly been a secret vocabulary established to guard against being recorded saying anything which could be used in a court of law. He'd been given limited information, with most conversations between Pedro and Juan happening in Spanish. Without his phone, he was unable to document the bags of cocaine wrapped in plastic and concealed beneath the coconuts and mangoes.

It was close to 3:00am when he was instructed to anchor a short distance from Cape Conway National Park. The *fish*, which was the term they used instead of drugs, had been loaded into two backpacks that Juan and Scott would carry to the designated rendezvous point. Fred transported the two men and *the fish* ashore in a small dinghy with an outboard motor. There were no other vessels around and the only sounds were coming from the birdlife in the bush and the gentle lapping of the water against the shore. Scott estimated each backpack weighed around thirty kilos. They were difficult to pick up. Scott helped Juan adjust his load and in doing so spotted a pistol on his belt. Juan glared at him.

'For the crocodiles,' he said, too quickly. Scott realised there was maybe less chance of him being alive at the end of the day than he'd first assumed.. He felt confident that he could escape in the bush, but he had no way of contacting Charlotte to tell her she was in danger. And for how long would they need to do this? He imagined that Pedro had a large network. No. He had to learn enough about the operation to bring it down.

Small wallabies, possums, scrub fowl and brush-turkeys bounced and crashed through the undergrowth as they made their way along a creek bed and then up onto higher ground. As daylight filtered down through the thick canopy, they arrived in an area surrounded by sandstone boulders.

'Sit. We wait here,' Juan instructed. Scott was pleased to get the heavy load off his back and moved over to lean against one of the rocks, taking in his surroundings. 'Not there. Here,' Juan commanded, pointing to a large tree with his left hand with the gun pointed directly at Scott's temple.

'What?' Scott yelled.

'Gatos may trust you. But I do not.'

'Call him.'

'It is not possible. And I have Gatos' blessing to dispose of you if I have doubts.'

Scott quietly complied, sitting down where instructed, and was tied to the tree with a rope that Juan took from his backpack. Confident that the Australian was secured, Juan retrieved a two-way radio from the front of his pack and walked back down the path. For the first time in a long while, Scott had no idea what to do next.

9

CHARLOTTE: TUE 9 FEB 8:00AM

Charlotte was pacing the deck at the marina when Kirra arrived the following morning.

'Any news?' Charlotte asked anxiously.

'Maybe,' Sergeant Sillago said quietly. 'You had coffee yet?' Charlotte shook her head and followed the officer below deck.

She took the same seat in the lower cabin where she'd been interviewed the previous day. Kirra flipped open her notebook and offered a friendly smile. The notebook had a beautiful Aboriginal fabric cover, like those Charlotte had seen in Yindi's boutique the day before.

'Let's start at the beginning. How long have you known Scott Harmon?'

'Most of my life,' Charlotte replied.

'And how long has he been involved with the yachting community?'

'Since he left university and went overseas. So about five years. Prior to that he was a keen surfer and occasional life saver.'

'And where did he visit overseas?'

'Many places. He's been to the Caribbean, France, Italy and most recently Vanuatu.'

'Did he ever go to Central America, say to Panama for example? It's not too far from the Caribbean.'

'He's never mentioned that to me.'

'Or has he spent time sailing out of Newport in Sydney?'

'You'd have to ask him when we find him. Do you have any news?' At that moment, the radio on the boat crackled and interrupted their conversation. Charlotte tapped her fingernails on the arm of the seat while Kirra took the call. Something big was happening, as evidenced by the number of *Ah Has* and *I See* Kirra offered while notes were furiously scribbled. Ten minutes later the call ended. Kirra flipped back to her first page and looked at Charlotte.

'I have news. The yacht *Ojo Del Tigre* has been located.'

'What a relief. Is Scott OK?'

'He was not aboard.'

'What! I don't believe it,' Charlotte said.

'They looked everywhere. There were only two people aboard.'

'Isn't that suspicious? Surely a crew of two isn't enough? They didn't look hard enough. He could have been tied up in the hold.'

'Trust me. They looked everywhere. The officers inspecting the yacht were from the Drug Squad. They know how to search a vessel.' Charlotte suddenly remembered Teal's words of warning the previous evening.

'How closely was the yacht being monitored? Did anyone see anything suspicious or anybody leaving the yacht? By boat or helicopter?'

Kirra looked at the computer screen and then back to Charlotte.

'I'm not able to share information regarding an ongoing investigation.' Charlotte shook her head and picked up her bag. Kirra returned her attention to the screen. 'Wait a second. He's been found. He's a passenger on a flight from Bundaberg into Proserpine. Due to land in an hour.'

'Thank you. But that doesn't make any sense. Why would he fly back to Bundaberg from Hamilton Island and then up to Proserpine? Do you know when the next ferry departs for the mainland?'

'Not for a couple of hours, but if you don't tell anyone, we can give you a ride to Shute Harbour and you can grab a cab from there. We're leaving in five.'

'Yes please. Accepted with thanks.'

It was a beautiful day for a trip on the water. A few fluffy clouds were nudged by gentle winds across a deep blue sky. As the police boat left the marina, Charlotte relaxed a little. Scott would be able to answer her questions and she'd soon be chastising herself for having worried unnecessarily. She looked across at Kirra, who had binoculars focused on the lush mountainous foreshore.

'See anything unusual?'

'A handful of fishermen who haven't anchored their boats thoughtfully. They need to be tied to the designated buoys so they don't disturb the ocean floor.'

'It certainly is lush. What's the area called?'

'It's the Conway Ranges and is now a National Park. The traditional owners include the Birri-Gubba Nation and the Gia and Ngaro mobs. My grandfather was an Ngaro elder and one of the best trackers in the area.'

'Reckon you'd need a tracker to navigate that bushland.'

'Too right you would. There are a few tracks but most of the cape is unsuitable for hiking – and there's a couple of things you need to look out for – like stinging trees and red-bellied blacksnakes. And for younger folk, there's quite a bit of distress in visiting the park because of the limited mobile phone coverage.'

'Are there any trackers left?' Kirra hesitated.

'No. Not really. My grandfather's mate Nev, *Nonsense Nev*, used to be a tracker, but he's not done that for years. He's a fisherman now.'

'Why's he called Nonsense?'

'Because of irony. He's a crusty character and takes no prisoners if you know what I mean. So the name Nonsense has stuck. He doesn't mind.' Charlotte gazed across at the foreshore and then turned to Kirra, asking her what had made her join the police force.

'There was a campaign to recruit more indigenous officers. I liked the recruiting officer I spoke to and the opportunity to stay and work in the local area was enticing. And my dad, who's a park ranger, thought it would be a good idea too.'

Charlotte's phone rang, and Kirra moved across to speak to the officer driving the boat.

'Hi C. How's things?' Miranda asked.

'Interesting. This is a lovely part of the world.'

'Is Scott with you?'

'Um. No. Not at the moment. But I'm just coming in to pick him up now.'

'Good. Can you tell him to turn his jolly phone on? He's driving Mason crazy.'

'Will do. Off to see him now, I'll pass on your instructions. Gotta go, Miranda. Bye.'

Kirra returned and took a seat on the bench cushion beside her. 'I have good news.'

'Yay? What?'

'Scott accepted a lift to Cannonvale Police station and is currently assisting the team there with their enquiries.'

'Enquiries about what?' Charlotte asked. Kirra hesitated. She was clearly uncomfortable disclosing the nature of the investigation.

'Related to the search of the yacht Scott was meant to be on?'

'Perhaps. And other things,' Kirra replied quietly. 'You'll need to ask him.'

A police car was waiting for them near the port and fifteen minutes later Charlotte followed Kirra into the police station. She took a seat in the waiting area and started reading the different notices.

'Scott Harmon, you've got a visitor,' a voice announced from behind the reception desk. Charlotte was not sure who was more surprised when the person assisting police enquiries sauntered into the reception.

'Hello darling. Thanks for coming to get me.'

'Who the hell are you?'

'Don't talk like that, love. I know I'm late. People are watching.' He theatrically walked over to kiss her and she pushed him away.

'This is not Scott Harmon,' Charlotte announced loudly, looking at the person in front of her, who was enjoying the case of mistaken identity. Charlotte could see that this imposter shared a similar build and height to

Scott and also had his dirty blonde hair, pulled back in a tiny ponytail.

'It seems Australia has two Scott Harmons,' Kirra said. 'His driver's license checks out.' Charlotte shook her head.

'I'm relieved this wasn't my Scott, but now I'm even more anxious about where he is. Can we discreetly file a missing person's report? I don't want his parents or sister to know anything's amiss.'

'Look, Charlotte. You've no evidence that he's come to harm. Dare I suggest that he's gone off with someone else and doesn't want to be found?' Charlotte took a deep breath and shook her head.

'I can see why you'd think that. And certainly, that would be a possibility if Scott wasn't Scott.' She glared at the other Scott Harmon who was now standing outside the police station smoking. 'He wouldn't muck me around like that and it's totally inconsistent with his last message. More telling is the fact that he's not been in touch with his sister or best friend. They're getting married in eleven days.'

'Here's what we'll do. At 4:00pm today, which is officially twenty-four hours after you expected to see him, I'll file a missing person's report. If you don't mind coming with me while I shout at a few fishermen near Cape Conway, we'll give you a lift back to Hamilton Island. He may well turn up with flowers and an amusing explanation for his unexplained absence.'

'I hope so. Thank you, Kirra. And yes, I'll accept your kind offer of another taxi ride back to Hamilton Island.'

'Let's grab a coffee and something to eat first.'

. . .

In the nearby café, Charlotte pulled out the notebook in which she'd been scribbling down questions the previous evening. She started summarising what she knew as fact, what was suspicion and what she needed to know.

Kirra returned to the table and smiled.

'You've been to Mum's shop?'

Charlotte looked up, surprised. 'Yindi's your mother?'

'Yep. And my best friend.'

'She's a wonderful artist and I think I could create beautiful outfits from the fabric, a bit more formal than the t-shirt and sarong combinations she's already created.'

'How lovely. Already excited to see what you come up with.'

'Give me an email or phone number and I'll send you a photo.' Kirra passed Charlotte a business card, stood up quickly and put her hat on. A shout outside had caught her attention. As they emerged from the café, they could see a crowd of around twenty people standing outside the office of the local member of parliament Bill Cowboy, with placards announcing *Not on our land, Never Ever, Frack off* and *Bill's a fraud*. Bill himself was trying to get them to disperse. They were not complying. As he pushed his rusty coloured hair down underneath a large Akubra hat he noticed them walking towards the protest.

'Kirra,' he cried out.

'Bill.'

'Keep an eye on this crowd for me, mate.'

'As always, Bill.' Charlotte and Kirra watched him squeeze his sizeable frame into his SUV, lavishly adorned with stickers saying *Bill is Best*.

'I guess the words *Humble* and *Bill* don't appear in the same sentences in the local newspaper very often.'

'You're right there Charlie Girl ,' Kirra said as the

police van depart for the marina. Charlotte was momentarily taken back by the informal way that Kirra had addressed her. Scott was the only person who called her *Charlie Girl.*

Her head was spinning as she sat on the bench at the back of the police launch. There was a beautiful view across the harbour, but she was unable to enjoy it because she had an underlying fear gnawing at her. Maybe, logically, it made sense to assume Scott was safe and sound somewhere, but she wasn't convinced. As she waited for the boat to depart, she watched the *Ojo del Tigre* slide into a nearby berth. The two police officers on her vessel were also studiously watching its arrival. Moments later, the other Scott Harmon sauntered up the pier, threw his cigarette into the water and walked aboard the yacht. He was cordially greeted by a man of medium height with a tanned complexion and Charlotte assessed that these people had not met before. The gang plank was pulled up and the two men went inside. Ten minutes later, the police vessel departed. They travelled close to the shoreline and Kirra made frequent use of the binoculars to scan the shores.

'Speak of the devil,' she muttered before putting her fingers in her mouth and ejecting a whistle that would have won a medal at any Olympic event. A lone fisherman gave a slow, high wave.

'Hey Nonsense. How're the fish biting?' she called across the water.

'Come and have a look yourself.'

The boat headed into shore and Kirra jumped into the shallow water and strolled up to and then hugged Nonsense Nev. She turned to Charlotte, who was still on the boat, and waved her in.

'I know what you're having for dinner tonight,' Kirra said, looking in his bucket. 'Come look what he's caught, Charlotte.' She turned back to Nev. 'Seen any trouble?'

'Guess you're here to sort out those blokes who don't know how to anchor proper,' he said pointing to half a dozen small watercraft in the distance.

'Yep. We've got them in our sights. Anything else?'

'Someone's left rubbish up yonder,' he said pointing at the hill behind him. 'Didn't see who it was.' Kirra nodded.

'Righteo. Can I leave Charlotte here with you for thirty minutes while I sort out this mob? She doesn't need to hear our conversation.' Nev nodded. 'That OK with you Charlotte?'

'Absolutely. It's beautiful here.'

'Charlotte's interested in how trackers spot signs. Think you could give her a few insights?' Kirra asked.

'Maybe,' Nev said noncommittally. Charlotte watched them cast off and head over to the first boat. She loved the feel of the crunchy sand under her feet. She walked and then ran and then performed a spontaneous cartwheel. Remembering the joy she'd had doing these as a child, she attempted three in a row and ended up landing in the shallows. She sat down and ran her hands through the sand, rich with broken coral, while looking out across the aquamarine-coloured water. Finding a smooth pebble, she stood up and skipped it across the water in three beautiful bounces. There were two slow moving objects in the water and she was delighted to watch two rays break the surface and then dive down along the sandy floor. The policeboat was now heading back to shore. Walking back towards Nev, she kicked up the sand and was startled when her toe caught on a string of beads that flicked high into the air. Scooping them up, she shook off the sand and shrieked. She was certain that the leather wristband belonged to Scott.

'What's up?' Kirra asked, wading ashore.

'I've just found these beads. I'm sure they belong to Scott. I'm certain he was here.'

'Every second surfer has a set of beads like that. Is there something unique about these?' Charlotte turned the beads over in her hand. It was true that other surfers wore beads with similar configurations to these on their wrists or ankles. But she had a strong feeling that these were his.

'I wanna go looking for him,' Charlotte said, pointing behind to the bush.

'That isn't practical. You shouldn't go alone. There's only six hours of daylight left and you're meant to have a permit. I can't ask for resources to look for him based on a feeling. We need stronger evidence than some beads. Sorry, Charlotte. We have to head back to Hamilton Island.'

'I'll take her,' Nev said quietly.

'Thank you,' Charlotte replied quickly, before Kirra could comment.

'You sure, Nonsense?' Kirra asked. He winked at her, and after a moment she sighed and nodded. 'OK then. Pay attention to what he tells you,' she said to Charlotte. 'He knows what he's doing. And don't get lost.' They both watched Kirra slowly wade back through the shallow water to the policeboat. As the boat headed back to Hamilton Island, Kirra waved and Nev went down to the water's edge and released the fish he'd caught.

'I'll come back for these tomorrow,' he said. Charlotte picked up his bucket and fishing line, leaving Nev free to scan the edge of the beach dunes for footprints.

'How big is your Scott?'

'About the same size as you?'

'Hmmm,' he replied.

'What do you see?' Charlotte asked nervously.

'Footsteps from two big blokes dragging their feet 'cause they're fat, or two smaller men with a heavy load.' Nev signalled for her to follow and put his fingers to his lips, indicating the need to travel quietly. They were soon deep in the rainforest with the sounds of brush-turkeys and scrub fowl running through the leaf litter, giving Charlotte the jitters, but not as much as the prehistoric looking lace monitors sitting quietly on the lower tree branches.

They came across a damp gulley, divided by a narrow stream. Ned encouraged her to have a drink while he scoured the area for broken twigs and snapped foliage. He squatted on his haunches to get a closer look at the ground.

'Careful where you step,' he said pointing at the slightest of trails through the mud. 'Red-bellied black snake nearby.' Charlotte immediately regretted not having worn socks with her sneakers.

'How do you know that's a red-bellied black snake's trail?' she whispered.

'Look. It's been shedding,' he said, pointing to a snake-skin that had been caught in an enormous spider's web and was gently waving in the breeze. Charlotte involuntarily gulped and watched where she placed her next step. The sounds of birdlife high in the trees were unfamiliar to her. It was a noisy chorus and she was sure that they were sending signals far and wide, warning others to beware as there were hunters below.

'The birds see you and hear you, and so will whoever's

with your friend.' Nev bent down, mixing soil with water in the palm of his hand, before smearing the mixture on her face. He also placed a ring of vines around her head and shoulders. 'No more talking, and you must walk gently and not disturb the earth.' Charlotte nodded and walked silently behind him, placing her feet exactly where he placed his. Moving higher up, they passed paperbacks and grasstrees before coming to an area where vines held the rainforest together. It was difficult to tell the time as Charlotte's phone had lost its signal and the further they moved under the rainforest canopy, the darker it got. Near a collection of boulders, Nev was able to confirm from markings on the ground, that two men carrying heavy backpacks had stopped there. Charlotte's spirits lifted.

'This is a sacred place. Those men have no right to be here,' he said softly.

10

SCOTT: TUE 9 FEB 2:00PM

Scott watched Juan talking on the two-way radio with whoever was coming to collect the drugs. It was a long conversation. While Juan was distracted, he tested the strength of the ropes that bound him to the tree. The knots were at the back and out of reach. He knew that by pulling hard he was tightening them and working against his objective of escape. He'd need to find another way. Juan's returning footsteps could be heard crunching the forest twigs.

'What's happening?' Scott asked. 'Where are they?'

Juan glared at him. 'There's been a delay.'

'Why?'

'You do not need to know,'

'Listen, matey. We're meant to be partners. We help each other.'

'You've carried *the fish* as required. How else could you possibly help me?'

'The Australian bush is full of danger.'

'Do not be ridiculous,' Juan snapped, lifting his revolver and aiming menacingly at Scott's head. 'I have this. And I have all I need.' Scott recognised that Juan was tired and that this was contributing to his volatility. He'd no idea how many hours had passed since they'd come ashore. Neither had slept for twenty-four hours. Scott leaned back against the tree, yawned and closed his eyes. He was tired as well, but his mind was racing, exploring scenarios in which he made it out of this predicament alive. His thoughts turned to Charlotte and he wondered what she was doing. He remembered the last time he'd seen her, the last time he'd held her, the last time he'd kissed her. Was it really only two weeks since he'd said goodbye to her at Krabi airport for a once-in-a-lifetime opportunity to sail from Port Vila to Bundaberg? If only he could go back in time and make a different decision. If only he'd chosen to stay longer with Charlotte.

His reverie was broken by the sound of nuts dropping. Well, that was what he thought he heard. He looked around and noticed something familiar on the leaf litter. It was his beaded leather wristband. When did it come off? No, wait. He'd taken it off on the balcony of the Reef Hotel when a sulphur crested cockatoo had started tapping on it with his beak. Then the cheeky blighter had flown away with his lucky charm. So the bird was here in the bush, watching him? Scott looked up into the rich tree foliage but couldn't see the white feathers of the thief with the distinctive yellow crest. Nor could he hear the bird's screechy cry. A branch dipped on a tree behind the now sleeping Juan. Scott focussed his eyes and was startled to see the whites of the eyes of an Aboriginal man. Was this the person coming to collect the drugs? Why wasn't he saying anything to announce his arrival?

The mysterious man pointed high up to another tree twenty metres away. Scott was staggered to see an Aboriginal woman curled up in the fork of two branches, not unlike a koala. She waved at him. Not the wave of a stranger, but of a friend. Scott stared back at the figure and suddenly realised it was Charlotte. His eyes flickered back to Juan to ensure he wasn't watching. His nemesis was still asleep. Scott's mind was racing as he looked back to the tree hosting his brilliant girlfriend. She was pointing at the backpacks. A carpet python lay coiled on top of the nearest one. That was convenient, Scott thought. He doubted Juan would know the difference between venomous and non-venomous snakes. He looked back at the now gently snoring Juan, who had a huge huntsman spider on his sleeve. The person accompanying Charlotte reached from behind a nearby bush and brushed Juan's face with a twig from a stinging tree, causing him to shout out in pain.

'Juan, there's a huntsman on your shirt.' Juan was confused, touching his face. It felt like hundreds of needles were piercing his skin. 'Forget your face, mate, flick the spider off before he bites you again.' Juan was distressed to see the large black spider crawling up towards his shoulder. He flailed his arms and the spider spun off into the bush from which it'd come. 'Let me have a look at your wound.' Juan walked closer to Scott and leant forward. 'Not good. Do you have antiseptic cream in your first aid kit?'

'What kit?' Juan replied.

'You mean you come into the Australian bush without a first aid kit? You're bloody stupid.' Juan's eyes drifted across to the backpacks and then he saw the python.

'What's that serpent?'

'Careful Juan. That's one of Australia's deadliest.' Juan

reached for his gun. 'Don't be an idiot. The noise will spook any nearby cassowaries.'

'What's that?'

'You don't know about the world's deadliest bird? They're taller than you and have a killer middle toe that can cut your throat or disembowel you – just like that,' he said clicking his fingers. Juan was unsettled and every noise in the bush was now causing him to look around in distress. 'Cut me loose and I'll remove the snake.' Juan moved quickly to untie the ropes securing Scott to the tree. Free of his bindings, Scott stood up and stretched, much to the annoyance of Juan.

'The snake,' Juan hissed. Scott walked slowly towards the carpet python, who regarded him for a moment before slipping off the backpack and into the bush. The snake had no interest in human contact. Turning around, Scott pretended to dust off his hands as though he'd been undertaking heavy labour. Juan glanced at the backpacks. 'It's gone?'

'Yes. It's gone. Why don't you go back down to the creek and wash your face? The cool water may help the stinging.' As Juan carefully made his way back down through the forest to the creek, Charlotte and Nev emerged from their hiding places.

'Scott, this is Nev,' Charlotte whispered.

'Thanks, Nev. The spider and snake. Pure genius,' he said, giving a thumbs up.

'You coming? He'll be back soon,' Charlotte said nervously.

'No. I want to get my eyes on the couriers and find out whatever else I can about...' Juan's terrified scream interrupted the conversation. Scott signalled for Charlotte and Nev to hide while he ran down to the creek. A small crocodile, no longer than thirty centimetres, had secured itself to Juan's hand.

'Get it off me,' Juan shouted.

'Shhhh. Wherever there's a baby croc, the mother's not too far away,' Scott said. The tiny reptile had a steel-like grip on his prey. Scott used his hands to cover the crocodile's eyes and the tiny creature involuntarily opened its mouth, dropping back into the creek. As they gingerly walked backwards away from the water, they could see bubbles emerging on the water's surface revealing the presence of a bigger beast below. Juan turned and ran, with Scott close behind him. On reaching the rendezvous point, Scott scrambled on top of the largest sandstone rock, and pulled Juan up. Scott wasn't sure if Juan was whimpering with pain from the crocodile bite or his brush with the stinging tree, or if the whole encounter with the spider and snake was what had really shattered his nerves. Blood was dripping from the wounds on his palm. Scott took off his t-shirt and wrapped it around Juan's hand. The snap of branches put them both on high alert and they watched nervously as two men in camouflage clothing arrived.

'Why didn't you answer your radio?' the taller of the two demanded.

'We were distracted, Bluey,' Juan replied.

'Where's Fred?' the man named Bluey asked.

'He hurt his hand,' Juan replied.

'Seems to be quite a bit of that going around,' Bluey observed, gesturing at Juan's hand. Juan shrugged.

'We've run into a bit of bad luck in the last twenty-four hours. What about you? Why are you late?'

'There are cops everywhere. We didn't want to risk being caught with the fish. Who's this?'

'Fred's replacement,' Juan said matter-of-factly.

'Where's the fish?' the other courier demanded.

'In a moment. Where's the bait?' Juan replied. Both men dipped their shoulders and swung their backpacks to the ground. Juan nudged Scott. 'Count it.' Scott slid off the rock and opened the first pack. There were hundred-dollar bills in packs of a hundred and dozens of packs in each bag.

'Hurry up. We've got to go.' Scott spent fifteen minutes counting the money, very aware that his fingerprints were now embedded on material likely to be presented as evidence in a court of law.

'You were expecting one point five million?' Scott asked Juan. He nodded and opened his palm, pointing to the other backpacks.

'This transfer is complete.' The men swapped back-packs and the camouflaged duo disappeared into the bush, as quickly as they arrived. Scott glanced through the tree foliage attempting to spot Nev or Charlotte.

'What are you looking for?' Juan demanded.

'Drop bears. I'd like to avoid them on the next leg of our journey.' Juan was bewildered and looked anxiously into the thick foliage. 'I've got your back, mate. Don't worry. More importantly, how're we getting to Airlie Beach?'

'There's a car parked on Brandy Creek Road. About two hours from here. We should make it in time for the rendezvous with the client this evening.'

'Who's the client?'

'Someone with land, who's happy for a cash sale.' Scott reached over and swung the first pack onto his back.

'Blimey. I guess I should be grateful that Pedro didn't

insist on payment in gold.' For the first time that day Juan smiled.

'Can you help me with the other one?' Scott nodded and carefully manoeuvred the pack up, avoiding Juan's damaged hand. 'Let's go,' Juan said impatiently as he scanned his surrounds for signs of bad-tempered birds, snap-happy crocodiles or previously unheard-of drop bears.

11

CHARLOTTE: TUE 9 FEB 4:00PM

Nev led Charlotte briskly through the bush for another hour until they came to a carefully graded path designed for visitor traffic.

'Easy from here. Walk to the end and you'll be on a road to town. OK?' Charlotte nodded as Nev melted back into the bush. As she moved closer to the end of the trail, she heard laughter and six people on Segways came rolling past. The scene was surreal. Her re-entry into civilisation was also confirmed by the ping of her phone and the presence of three signal bars and two messages. She immediately called Kirra and updated her on the events of the last three hours. Kirra was keen to come and collect her and would be there in five minutes. Charlotte slumped down onto the grassy verge and checked her messages from the bride-to-be.

Message from Miranda. *Major drama over where to seat Uncle Fred? Ideas?*

Message from Charlotte. *Why don't you give him his own table with responsibility for say music or master of ceremonies?*

Message from Miranda. *Music master is awesome idea. Mason is working on order of songs and all he'll need to do is hit play and stop – when he's told to. Taaa*

Message from Miranda. *Help! How can I stop Dad from sharing embarrassing stories about me in his speech?*

Message from Charlotte. *You worry too much. I really don't think he will, but I'll get Scott to check in with your Dad – just to be sure.*

Charlotte's phone rang, just as Scott and Juan emerged from the national park and started walking up the road. She concentrated on her call, ignoring them.

'Hi Mason. Where are you? Really? That's lucky because I'm near Airlie Beach too. Ah ha. Yep. That could work. I'll let you know where. Yes. I've been answering all Miranda's questions. Ah ha. OK. Gotta go. My ride's here. Talk soon.' Kirra had arrived in an unmarked police car. Charlotte climbed in and nodded towards the two men loading backpacks into the white sedan fifty metres up the road.

'That's unfortunate for them. Looks like a broken tail light.' Kirra swung the mobile police siren on to the roof and drove up beside the car which had pulled back onto the kerb.

'Afternoon gentlemen. Is this your car?' Scott was driving and took the lead in responding.

'A friend leant it to us.'

'Did you know you've got a broken tail light? And you stink. Where've you blokes been?' Kirra asked.

'Fishing.'

'Catch anything?'

'Nah. Too small. We let the little fellows go,' Scott replied.

'Good lads. Can you show me your fishing license?'

'We needed a license? Sorry.' Kirra regarded Scott and Juan carefully, noting the bloody shirt wrapped around his hand.

'What happened to your hand?'

'One of the fish bit me.'

'I thought that you said they were little fish. What type of fish caused an injury to generate so much blood? We don't have piranha in this country.'

'Must be the only type of dangerous animal that you don't have,' Juan hissed.

'What'dya say?' Kirra asked.

'Nothing,' Juan replied meekly. 'OK. It was a crocodile.'

'What! Now you're telling me whoppers. And if you're not, you'd better get on your way to the hospital to get a tetanus shot and possibly a few other needles. Crocs don't clean their teeth so they're full of rubbish. I'll give you a complimentary escort to the hospital. Follow me.'

'That'd be appreciated ma'am. Thank you,' Scott replied before turning to Juan, 'They should be able to give you something for that stinging cheek as well.'

Juan felt cornered, pissed off and overwhelmingly weary. He wanted to call Pedro but couldn't risk it with that policewoman around. He was also extremely uncomfortable that there was $1.5 million in the boot of the car. He'd have to trust that *crocodile whisperer* Scott while he went inside. The policewoman waited until Juan was in Outpatients before heading out of the car park and back to Airlie Beach.

'You OK to leave them unsupervised?' Charlotte asked.

'They're not unsupervised,' Kirra replied. 'You able to come back to the station now to make a statement?'

'You bet. And to share a few photos.'

'Good girl. You'd make a great spy.'

'I doubt it,' Charlotte replied dryly.

As they walked into the Airlie Beach police station Charlotte's phone rang. It was Miranda's mother, Jenny Harmon.

'Gotta take this,' Charlotte mouthed to Kirra.

'I'll go get coffee and sangas,' Kirra mouthed back.

'Hi Jenny,' Charlotte chirped into the phone.

'Hey Charlotte. We're at the bridal store now. We've whittled down the frock choices to two and now need your professional opinion.'

'My pleasure.'

Jenny Harmon turned the phone around to the small stage on which Miranda was modelling the first outfit. The first dress was in a vintage style with rustic lace and lantern sleeves.

'Hi C, what d'ya think?'

'It's lovely. And you look lovely in it. It's very traditional.'

'Rating out of ten?'

'I can't answer that. How do you feel wearing it?'

'It is lovely...' Miranda's voice trailed off.

'Try on the other one M,' Charlotte suggested while she walked outside to where it was quieter. The next dress was a sleeveless, sleek, modern, fitted v neck gown with a bustle drape.

'Wow,' Charlotte mouthed. 'That's one heck of a dress to make an entrance in. It'll take Mason's breath away.'

'Then this is it. I'll be taking it away today. Thanks C.'

'Pleasure. Gotta go.'

Kirra returned with cappuccinos and chicken salad sandwiches. While Charlotte devoured the much-needed sustenance, Kirra reviewed the photos Charlotte had taken from the tree. They featured an assortment of Akubra hats and baseball caps, hiding faces, which meant that it was difficult to identify anyone. There was however a clear shot of Scott counting money, which implicated him in the crime.

'Could you hear what they were saying?'

'Well, I did. But they were speaking a lot about fishing. Code I guess.'

'Probably. They're prepared in case someone was wired. Which is of course is exactly what we'd like to do. I wonder if we could get one on Scott. Would he be open to that?'

'Given that he's implicated in an international drug trading ring I think he'd be up for it. But how do we get to him? He's with the guy with the damaged hand,' Charlotte replied.

'I don't know yet. We'll need evidence and we'll want to catch the person at the top of the syndicate and not just the couriers.'

Charlotte's phone rang and Kirra signalled for her to take it, while she went into the next room.

'Hi Charlotte. I'm here. Where are you?' Mason asked.

'I'm having coffee with a friend for the moment.'

'What about Scotty? Where's he holed up?'

'He's at the hospital with a friend,' Charlotte replied.

'That would be why he's not returning my calls. Where's the hospital? I'll meet you there?'

'We're on the mainland. Why don't you catch the ferry over to Shute Harbour?'

'But aren't I meant to be doing the photo shoot and story about your artist here on Hamilton Island?'

'Yes. But that's tomorrow's story.'

'So what's today's story?'

'Man wrestles crocodile and survives.'

'Intriguing, but not really in the remit of *Hello*. Would it be an exclusive?' Mason asked.

'I'll do my best to keep it that way,' Charlotte said.

'Sold. On my way.'

Kirra returned and sat down beside Charlotte. 'They left the hospital twenty minutes ago and are parking at Airlie Beach,' she reported.

'I've an idea for how to record a possibly incriminating conversation. It's a bit wild. Do you wanna to hear it?' Charlotte asked an intrigued Kirra.

NEV: TUE 9 FEB 5:00PM

It was easy for Nev to follow the tall one and his chubby companion through the bush. They moved awkwardly and had to stop frequently to rest from the burden of carrying thirty kilos of cocaine each. They finally emerged onto farmland that skirted the national park. They moved quickly across an open field and then hid their backpacks in a banana packing shed before going inside a nearby house. Nev scaled a tree on the edge of the park to survey his surroundings. With open fields he could be easily spotted approaching the shed. There was still an hour of daylight left, so he decided to bide his time until darkness came while considering his next move. A smile slunk across his face as he considered the mischief he was about to create.

SCOTT: AN HOUR EARLIER TUE 9 FEB
4:00PM

'So you say a fish bit you?' the doctor asked sceptically. 'And several times?' Juan looked at Scott and said nothing. 'Those are not fish bites. Or certainly not from fish from this area.'

'Do you want me to tell you what we were really doing?' Scott asked.

'Up to you,' the doctor replied dryly as he stitched up the biggest gash.

'We might have been trying to get a closer look at a baby croc, and we were successful,' Scott said.

'Then you're both very lucky this is the only injury. You should report the location of the crocodile to the park ranger. Where was it exactly on the Cape?

'Couldn't tell you, Doc. It's a jungle in there and once we'd had our close encounter with the little snapper, we hot footed it out,' Scott replied.

'Smart move. There you go. Keep your hand dry.' Juan nodded to the doctor while watching the nurse as she administered a tetanus shot into his arm. 'Well, you've got a great story to tell your kids.'

'I don't think he's interested in telling anyone about our fishing trip,' Scott said attracting a curious stare from Juan.

The sun was setting as they walked across the hospital car park. 'You going to call Pedro to let him know where we are?' Scott asked. 'I don't have a phone.' Juan pulled the phone out of his pocket and waited till they were in the car before calling Pedro.

'En camino, (On the way),' Juan said simply before hanging up.

Pedro was smoking a cigar outside the Fish D'vine and The Rum Bar at Airlie Beach when Juan and Scott arrived twenty minutes later.

'Any problems?' Pedro asked. Scott looked at Juan, leaving him to choose how to reply.

'Nothing we couldn't manage,' Juan replied softly.

'Good. I've guests inside I'd like you to meet.'

Scott spotted the hat before he spotted the man. It spoke volumes that the man would choose to wear a hat called *the cattleman* indoors. Seated beside him was a younger man who in contrast, had dressed for invisibility in a fawn-coloured t-shirt and matching knee-length shorts. Pedro introduced Bill and Scott to Juan and Scott.

'We share the same name,' the invisible man remarked.

'Well, Scott is fairly common,' Scott replied.

'Not as common as Scott Harmon. I wished we shared girlfriends as well.'

'What!' Scott replied incredulously.

'Enough, enough,' Pedro instructed. Scott stared at the

man with the same name and wondered how he knew who Charlotte was.

'Scott, I'm going to need you to move that bait to Bill's vehicle. We're acquiring property from Mr Cowboy and setting up a barramundi fishing farm.' Scott had no idea what Pedro was talking about, but knew he was being asked to move the two backpacks that were currently in the boot of the car. Scott was reaching across to take the car keys from Juan when a familiar voice asked Juan,

'Are you the crocodile attack survivor?' Scott looked up and was startled to see Mason taking photos of everyone at the table. Mason leaned in with his microphone toward Juan, while surreptitiously placing a small recording device under the table. 'So how big was he?' Mason asked.

'I do not wish to speak about this incident,' Juan replied calmly.

'You were attacked by a crocodile? That's how you hurt your hand?' Pedro asked.

'It was very small. The injury is non-consequential,' he replied, before turning to Mason, 'you're interrupting a private meeting. Please leave.'

'So where'd it happen so I can warn everyone to keep away from the area?' Mason asked, ignoring the request.

'I don't remember and again, I am politely asking you to leave. Now.' Mason shrugged his shoulders and walked out of the bar. The people at nearby tables had stopped talking to watch the interaction. A few had started taking photos.

'Let's go back to the yacht,' Pedro said, in a tone which indicated that this was not a suggestion. As Pedro signalled for the bill the tall and chubby pair entered the bar and approached the table.

'Where is it?' the man known as Bluey demanded.

'Shhh,' Pedro hissed. 'Keep your voice down. What are you talking about?'

'The fish. Where are the fish?' Bluey said.

'We've already transferred them to you,' Juan said.

'They've gone missing,' Bluey hissed a little louder.

'That then would be your problem,' Juan replied.

'We want our bait back,' the chubby one said.

'No. The terms of the transfer have been followed,' Juan insisted.

'You must have a mole,' Bluey said, too loudly. He and his companion focussed their attention on Charlotte's Scott Harmon. Pedro looked at Juan, demanding an explanation.

'He was with me for the entire fishing trip,' Juan said. All eyes then turned to the other Scott Harmon, with the chubby one reaching across the table to grab his t-shirt.

'I know nothing about this. I'm the money man,' the other Scott shouted. This loud admission prompted an elbow to the jaw from Pedro, and suddenly fists were flying and chairs were being broken.

'I think I'll leave you gentlemen to sort this out,' said Bill Cowboy, throwing twenty dollars on the table before making a hasty exit.

'Anything we can help you with, Bill?' Kirra said, appearing out of thin air with a support team of four. 'We hear there's been an assault.'

'Nothing to do with me Kirra. I think there's been a simple misunderstanding between colleagues. Nothing to concern yourself with.'

'Thanks for that advice, Bill. Can I invite everyone back to the station with us for an informal chat, just to confirm you're all on the same page.' Glances were exchanged between Juan and Pedro and cautious nods offered. Mason continued to take photos as the seven men were led out of the bar to a large police van. Nothing was said in the van, but the glare of The Tiger reminded everyone of his deadly power.

Scott glanced at Charlotte, sitting in the reception area of the police station as he was directed through to an interview room. She was on the phone and gave him the slyest of looks as he walked past. It was reassuring knowing she was there.

14

CHARLOTTE: TUE 9 FEB 6:00PM

Charlotte's phone rang the moment she sat down in reception at the Cannonvale police station.

'So you got some good snaps?' Charlotte asked.

'My word I did,' Mason replied. 'This is going to be a ripper story. Can you speak? Are they there yet?'

'That is the case,' Charlotte replied watching the seven men arrive and be escorted in single file through to the back of the station. Scott looked at her momentarily as he walked past and she hoped furiously that he could read her mind. 'Work on your story and I'll call you when I know what's happening next.' Charlotte ended the call and her phone pinged, revealing messages from Miranda and her mother.

Message from Miranda. *Won't be able to fly to London with Mason as I need to wait for work visa. Feeling sad.* 😣

Message from Charlotte. *Don't worry. Will give Mason time to get your new home ready for you.*

Message from Miranda. *Mason tells me we'll have to live at his place in West Kensington with four other blokes, until I get a job and we can afford our own place. Thoughts?*

Message from Charlotte. 😯 *Apply for jobs immediately!*

Message from her mother. *Not seeing any photos from Hamilton Island. You and Scott haven't had a fight have you?*

Message to her mother. *Been having too much fun Mum. More soon.*

Message from her mother . *Honey. You know that you're meant to be organising the bridal shower event for Miranda?*

Message to her mother. *Groan. No. Any ideas?*

Message to Charlotte. *High tea at our house. Just immediate family and a few of Miranda and Mason's closest friends. Dad can probably put together a slide of Miranda growing up with Jenny's help. (We'll keep that secret). Great if you can send through a few photos too. How about a pass-the-parcel with questions about Miranda?*

Message to her mother. *Well, I couldn't play as I know everything.*

Message to Charlotte. *Agreed. Particularly as you'll be preparing all the questions.*

Message to her mother. *Thank you. You're a wonderful Mum.*

Message to Charlotte. 😵 *Don't mind. Just getting in the practice.*

Message to her mother. *Ignoring that* 😎

'Oh, hello there,' Charlotte said to a familiar face who'd just walked in to the station. 'What've you been up to, Nev?'

15

SCOTT: TUE 9 FEB 6:00PM

Scott felt like an hour had passed before the door to his interview room opened. It was so frustrating not having his phone. The female police officer placed a cappuccino and plate of sandwiches in front of him.

'I've been told you're probably hungry,' Kirra said.

'Thank you. It's been a while.'

Kirra smiled and told him, 'My colleague will join us shortly and we'll record our conversation.' The officer arrived and the recorder was turned on. 'This is Sergeant Kirra Sillago. I'm in interview room three with Corporal Sam Smith interviewing Scott Harmon of Byron Bay. Scott, can you please describe your movements over the last two days.'

'Can I go back a little bit further than that? It's important,' Scott asked.

'Of course. Go back as far as you need,' Kirra replied.

'It started with a wonderful job offer when I was on holiday with friends in Krabi. An opportunity to race from Port Vila to Bundaberg, in the stormy season.' Scott quickly described the events of the last couple of weeks. Kirra laughed when he described the things that Nev did with the spider and the snake to spook Juan. Scott clearly described his own role in counting the money and noted that his fingerprints on the notes would verify this. He hadn't met the politician Bill Cowboy before and knew nothing about the proposed land sale. The realisation that there was another Scott Harmon who was also a skipper, explained why Pedro Gatos had recruited him.

'So what happened tonight? Why did the local drug distributors blame you for stealing their stash?' Kirra asked.

'I'm not sure, but I have a feeling that that Aboriginal tracker was involved.' Kirra supressed a grin and turned off the recording.

'Thank you for that. We need to speak to the others and will probably come back to you with further questions. You're not leaving the area immediately, are you?'

'Does the area include Hamilton Island? I really want to spend some quality time with my Charlie Girl over there.'

'I'm over there myself tomorrow so we can get you to sign your statement then.'

'You beauty.'

Kirra walked out to the reception with Scott and was surprised to see Nev and Mason sitting on either side of Charlotte. Mason stood up and walked over to Kirra waving a USB storage device.

'There's a few photos and a recording on there that you may find of interest.'

'Wonderful,' she said reaching out to take it.

'Not so fast,' Mason replied, closing the USB back within his palm.

'What do you want?' Kirra replied suspiciously.

'I'm doing a photo shoot with your Mum tomorrow. Would you be open to being included in a couple of shots?'

'Is that all?' she asked.

'And could I interview you for an article I'm writing: 'How we caught *The Tiger.*'

Kirra regarded him carefully. 'Yes, to your first request and we'll see about the second one. We need to be confident that we've everything we need to bring this cartel down. However, when we reach that point, you're welcome to ask me again.'

'Perfect,' Mason replied dropping the USB drive into Kirra's open hand.

'Now. You three skedaddle. I need to have a chat with Nev. Thanks for your efforts today.' She shook their hands and while Scott wrapped Charlotte in his arms, Mason watched Nev and Kirra walk out the back together.

'I bet that Nev's got a story.'

'Guarantee it,' Charlotte replied as her phone pinged with another message from Miranda.

- *Cake* ✓
- *Menu* ✓
- *Seating plan* ✓

It's all coming together. Have you got your dress?

Charlotte texted back

Soon!

'Excuse me. I'm on my way to Shute Harbour and I've been told you might like a ride,' Corporal Smith said, shaking a set of car keys.

'That's very kind of you,' Mason replied. 'What a wonderful service.'

'I was going anyway as I have to pick someone up.'

Scott was not surprised to see Fred the chef in handcuffs standing beside another police officer at the marina. Fred snarled and then spat at Scott as he walked towards the police officer.

'Lovely to see you again too, Fred.'

'Can I pop back onto the yacht to get my phone?' Scott asked the policeman.

'Afraid not. It's a crime scene now. What does your phone look like?'

'Like most other phones, I guess. Black. Samsung. Ah. And there's a screen saver of my gorgeous girlfriend,' he said, pointing at Charlotte. The policeman put his hand in his pocket and pulled out a plastic bag with a phone inside. He touched the screen and looked at the image.

'Indeed. She is lovely. But I can't give this to you. This has been bagged as evidence. If Sergeant Sillago says it's OK, you can collect it tomorrow.'

'Brilliant, thank you.'

They boarded the transfer boat to Hamilton Island with dozens of other tourists. Mason immediately took a seat and started tapping out a story on his tablet. Charlotte took a call from her mother and Scott leaned against the guard rail, staring back at the *Ojo Del Tigre*. It struck him how lucky he was to have gotten off the yacht alive.

'Penny for your thoughts,' Charlotte said as she gently leant against him. He put his arms around her and kissed her forehead.

'My thoughts are worth more than pennies. They're worth even more than gold. I'm so lucky to have you in my life, and I'm so looking forward to having that quality time together we promised ourselves.'

'Now I need you to hold on to that thought, as I have bad news.' Scott's heart skipped a beat as he examined her face for signs that she was joking. 'I really have to go home tomorrow. There are so many things I need to do to make sure that your sister's wedding to your best friend is as magical as it should be. Miranda's upset because she won't be able to leave for London with Mason as she needs to wait for a work visa. Do you think you can come back with me?'

'I don't know. I need to make sure the police have everything they need to convict Pedro. We need him behind bars. It's also likely that Nev and I will need to show them where the drug exchange happened on the Cape. I'll know more tomorrow. We've still got tonight?'

'And we've got company...' Charlotte replied, looking at Mason.

They all agreed they were too tired to go out for a celebratory dinner back on Hamilton Island. Instead, they picked up fish and chips wrapped in newspaper to eat on the terrace. As they opened the wrapping of the steaming feast, half a dozen sulphur crested cockatoos swooped in.

'You little thieves,' Scott said attempting to shoo them

away. Charlotte chuckled while Mason took photos. 'Now which one of you little blighters stole my wrist band?'

'Hang on?' Charlotte said. 'One of these guys took your lucky band and dropped it on the beach at Conway? It wasn't you leaving me a clue?'

'That would have been remarkable foresight on my behalf. But alas, it wasn't me.'

'Have another chip then,' Charlotte said, opening up the newspaper for her feathered friends. She turned to Mason who was still snapping images. 'That's probably enough, Mason.'

'Don't you get it? This story just got even more interesting. Not only do we have the leader of a drug syndicate called Tiger and an Aboriginal tracker called Nonsense but now a cheeky cracker of a cockatoo whose thieving activities gave you the incentive to go into the *dangerous* Australian bush to rescue the love of your life. Wow. This story is going to go viral, and I'm the only one with all the pictures and a close relationship with the people at the centre.'

'My word Mason. You should consider writing fiction rather than writing for *Hello*.'

'Who knows what opportunities this story will generate,' Mason replied, popping another hot chip in his mouth.

Scott made up the sofa bed for Mason while Charlotte showered. All was quiet when she tiptoed out of the bathroom fifteen minutes later, except for the sound of the two men gently snoring.

CHARLOTTE: WED 10 FEB 7:00AM

S cott was still asleep when Charlotte reached for her phone the next morning and pulled it back under the covers.

Message from Miranda . *Am nervous it might rain. Ideas?*

Message from Charlotte. *Buy 20 silver umbrellas. Will make for a beautiful photo if it does. BTW. I'm flying home today.*

Message from Miranda . *Yay. Will pick you up from airport.*

Message from her mother. *How's Scott?*

Message from Charlotte. *Asleep*

Message from her mother. *What have you been doing?*

Message from Charlotte. *Bush walking. Boat rides. Taking photos of wildlife. Usual stuff.*

Message from her mother. *Any other news?*

Charlotte knew her mother was prodding for news of a potential engagement.

Message from Charlotte. *Yes. I'm coming home early.*

Message from her mother. *Alone?*

Message from Charlotte. *Yes. Scott has stuff to do.*

Message from her mother. *Stuff?*

Message from Charlotte. *Paperwork related to the yacht cruise.*

Message from her mother. *Shall I collect you from the airport?*

Message from Charlotte. *No. Miranda's got me covered.*

'Who are you texting?' Scott whispered as he nibbled her ear.

'Usual suspects. My mother. Your sister.'

'Put the phone down and give me your attention please.'

'You beauty!' came a cry from the living room. 'Guess what guys? My photo and story from the bust-up last night are on the front page of the *Whitsunday Times*. Come and look.' Charlotte and Scott slipped on their matching white cotton, hotel bathrobes and joined Mason on the sofa, reading the paper now spread out across the coffee table.

Bill Cowboy comes to blows in bar fight

Seven men were involved in an altercation last night at the Rum Bar on Airlie Beach. Several tables and chairs were broken. Police officers were quickly on the scene, relocating all involved to the Cannonvale police station for further questioning. No information relating to the source of the disturbance has been released by the police although local member Bill Cowboy commented that he hardly knew the people he was dining with and had only been invited to advise on land values.

There was an emotion-rich photograph of the chubby one pulling the other Scott Harmon to his feet by his t-shirt, while Bill Cowboy looked on horrified.

'Very pleased that I'm not in the photo and let me state categorically, that the only photo I wish to appear in, is at your wedding,' Scott said.

'That's it?' Mason asked.

'That's it,' Scott replied.

Yindi hung the *Back in a couple of hours* sign on the door of her gift shop while Scott placed her suitcase with several outfits in the back of a taxi with Charlotte's bag. Kirra was already at the One Tree Hill viewpoint when they arrived five minutes later. There was a beautiful view across the aquamarine bay to nearby islands. Charlotte quickly captured a few memories on her phone.

'Thirty minutes only,' Kirra said to Mason, tapping her watch. With Charlotte's assistance he quickly moved Kirra and her mother through different costume changes and backdrops, all the while asking them about their motivation for choosing their respective careers. When Kirra announced time was up, Mason thanked them and let them know the expected release date of the mother-daughter story in *Hello*. Their taxi dropped Yindi back at the Reef Hotel, Charlotte at the airport and Kirra, Mason and Scott at the marina where the police launch was waiting to ferry them back to Airlie Beach. As Charlotte looked out the window of the small plane as it ascended into the azure sky, she was sure she could see Scott looking up at her from the deck of the boat.

17

SCOTT: WED 10 FEB 10:00AM

Scott's heart sank as he watched Charlotte's plane fly overhead. Their plans for a romantic trip together had been ruined. The last three days had felt like thirty. He wanted her on his own, preferably with no phone contact with the outside world. Just the two of them. Yes. Having had his phone returned by Kirra as he boarded the launch, he quickly texted Charlotte as they pushed off from Hamilton Island.

'You OK?' Kirra asked.

'Am I OK? Well, I'm a bit lovesick to be honest and wishing I was on that plane,' he said, pointing at the sky.

'Thanks for staying longer. We'll make good use of your time. It'll be a busy day, though, what with reviewing your statement, retracing your journey through the Cape and an interview early evening,' Kirra said.

'Another interview? With who?'

'Dunno. Someone from Interpol. Not surprising given the reach of Gatos' network. We expect to charge them today and we'll remand them in custody until the trial. The yachts have been impounded and arrests in Port Vila and Panama are imminent. Saying it's a good result is an understatement.'

Kirra was accosted by several journalists upon arrival at the station.

'Can you give us more details about the drug bust, Kirra?'

'I expect to be able to make a formal statement tomorrow folks,' she replied before walking inside. Mason sat in reception working on his fashion story while Kirra and Scott went back to an interview room to review his statement. Emerging twenty minutes later they were pleased to see Nev chatting with Mason.

'Can I get a photo of you two?' Mason asked Kirra.

'What about Scott?' she replied.

'He's camera shy and says I already have a photo of one Scott Harmon which is more than enough,' Mason said.

'Let's do it on the boat.' Kirra said. Mason agreed, and she turned to Nev.

'I'll need your help to track the route – you'll have to show me where the exchange took place, where the stash was hidden and where you moved it to.'

Nev tilted his head, acknowledging the request.

An hour later they were wading through shallow water to arrive at the small beach where Charlotte first discovered Scott's wrist band. Without the need to carry a thirty-kilo backpack, the group of four moved swiftly from the beach and through the undergrowth. When they reached the creek where Juan had had his encounter with the baby crocodile, Mason insisted on taking several photos at the water's edge, attracting warning screeches from nearby bird life and a speedy exit away to the sandstone boulders where the drug transfer had taken place. More photos were taken as Nev identified the tree where Scott was secured and where Charlotte and he had watched the unfolding activities from on high. Mason asked Nev to describe again what he did to spook Juan, capturing his sense of mischief on film. This material was not considered evidentiary, so Mason was given permission to share it. Finally, they visited the banana packing shed, where Nev had taken the drugs from, and a dilapidated farm vehicle parked two hundred metres from the farmhouse, which was where he'd hidden them. Kirra called her colleagues, and a car was sent to drive them back to the police station. Mason was deeply engrossed, writing on his tablet throughout the journey back, occasionally chuckling to himself, much to the amusement of the others. Upon arrival Mason took his now familiar seat in reception, while Scott and Nev went out the back to the interview rooms. Scott was surprised to see an elegantly dressed and perfectly coiffed grey-haired woman waiting for him in interview room one.

'How do you do Scott. My name's Teal. Teal Dubois.'

'And you're from Interpol.'

'Not exactly, but that's close enough. Thanks for being available to meet with me. I've reviewed your statement and want to explore a few more areas.'

'Fire away,' Scott replied. For the next hour Teal peppered Scott with questions about both yachting trips and the conversations he'd with Pedro, Juan and Fred. Scott didn't think he provided any additional insights, but the curious woman seemed satisfied.

'What are your plans now?' she asked, closing her notebook.

'To spend more time with my girlfriend.'

'I meant your goals for say the next six to twelve months,' Teal clarified.

'I'll look around for another yachting gig, this time doing a bit more homework about who's employing me. Longer term I'd like to buy my own yacht and charter it out.'

'I see. I may have an opportunity for you,' she said.

18

CHARLOTTE: WED 10 FEB 11:30AM

The moment the plane's wheels kissed the tarmac in Brisbane, Charlotte turned on her phone to see Scott's message.

Watching you fly away is breaking my heart. Soon. I'll be back in Brisbane very soon.

She smiled and put her phone away. She'd need to focus now on bridesmaid duties. Pulling out the notebook she'd bought in Yindi's shop, Charlotte started writing down a to-do list for the bridal shower based on her conversation with her Mum the previous day.

- Confirm date for shower as Valentine's Day. How perrrfect
- Decide who to invite
- Send invitations and apologise for short notice
- Organise music, games and activities – *not boring ones*
- Decide on food – super yummy only

- Prepare Miranda and Mason's magical love
  story ❤

Those are the main things for the shower, Charlotte thought to herself. What else is there to do?

- Buy bridesmaid dress
- Buy wedding present
- Do anything else bride needs
- Supervise boyfriend being fitted for suit

Boyfriend she thought to herself. Will need to confirm arrival time tomorrow so can collect from airport.

'Hey C,' came Miranda's voice from the other side of the luggage carousel.

'Hey there M. How's things? Any news on the visa?' Charlotte asked as she hugged her friend.

'No, not yet. Probably another three weeks,' Miranda replied, sucking in her bottom lip.

'Then let's keep you super busy so the time flies,' Charlotte said.

'That will be so easy. There are a million things to do.'

'Well, the bridal shower is in mine and Mum's hands. I won't be sharing any of the details with you.'

'Not even a little bit?'

'Nope,' Charlotte replied.

'Well, can you tell me what the deal was with the cockatoos?'

19

SCOTT: THU 11 FEB 7:00AM

Thursday morning Mason woke to news that his fashion story with Yindi and Kirra had been well received at the offices of *Hello*. More excitingly for him, the cockatoo story was running viral.

Crafty cockatoo leaves vital clue on Cape Conway

A sulphur crested cockatoo has helped reunite lovers. A wrist band which was stolen and then dropped by a cheeky bird at the beginning of a pathway into Cape Conway National Park revealed the direction that a Brisbane woman's boyfriend had taken to go fishing. When he didn't return at the appointed hour, she set off to find him. Discovery of the beaded leather band on the foreshore prompted her to head inland. The woman's partner was discovered two hours later leaning up against a tree. Pleased to have been found, the man has said that in future he will take his girlfriend fishing with him.

'What a load of nonsense Murray,' Scott said before he

hit him with a fluffy pillow. 'The leaning up against a tree is clearly code for *drunk as a skunk*. You're killing my reputation.'

'What are you upset about, Harmon? There's no photo of you or name reveal. And you did go fishing,' Mason retorted, before adding, 'it was challenging to write the piece without revealing the bigger story about the drug for dosh exchange.' Scott started scrolling through the comments at the bottom of the article.

What a galah!
No wonder your names aren't revealed.
'Who's a clever cocky then?'

Scott's phone rang. It was Charlotte.

'Yes, I've seen it. Yes, I've hit him with a pillow. Yes, he's still smiling. Yes, that's right. Landing just before noon. Me too.'

'I've acquired another 18,000 followers overnight,' Mason reported gleefully.

'That's wonderful mate. Pick up your bag, we've a plane to catch.' Mason's eyes remained fixed on his phone for the next hour. They'd just arrived at the airport when Mason became even more excited.

'Kirra's just held a press conference announcing the arrest of six men with drug trafficking and money laundering charges.'

'I don't get why you're so excited?'

'Because now I can release my crocodile story.' Before Scott could respond his phone rang. He listened without speaking, said 'I understand' and then rang off. 'Mate. I've gotta take a different flight. There's something I've gotta do.'

'Your girlfriend's going to be pissed.'

'She'll understand. Eventually.'

'You're engaging in risky behaviour.'

Scott hesitated before replying. 'See you at the wedding.'

'You're not coming back until the day of the wedding?' Mason said incredulously.

'I'll try. Can you get my suit sorted out? Just in case?'

20

CHARLOTTE: THU 11 FEBRUARY
10:00AM

'Now don't be mad with me,' Scott pleaded.

'You're not flying back today, are you?' Charlotte said.

'That's correct.'

'You've taken another sailing job?'

'How did you know?'

'Stab in the dark. And you've double checked that the owner of the boat is one hundred percent legit?'

'Yes. They don't have a criminal record,' Scott answered, suppressing a smile.

'So when will I see you?'

'Depends on sailing conditions, but ...' he hesitated.

'When?' Charlotte demanded.

'The 19th February.'

'Blimey, Scott. Your sister and best friend are getting married on the 20th. That's in nine days' time. You're cutting it more than a little close. And you'll miss the bridal shower,' she added for emphasis.

'Isn't that only for women?' he asked, a little confused.

'Well, yes, normally, but because there's no time for a

bridal shower and a rehearsal dinner we're combining them. Your grandparents are coming.'

'I'll see them at the wedding.'

'Scott Harmon. I need to hang up now as I'm so annoyed with you. But before I do you need to promise to call me every day.'

'I'll try,' he replied.

'What do you mean you'll try?' Charlotte replied angrily.

'Well, I'll try. It does of course depend on internet access.'

'Is there anything else you need to tell me?' There was a moment's silence on the line.

'Nothing I want to tell you over the phone. But when I get back...'

'Alright then. Bye Scott.'

'Bye Charlie Girl .'

21

MASON: THU 11 FEB 11:45 AM

It was lovely to see Miranda in the airport arrival halls. Mason noted that her face flickered between delight and concern and he already knew what she'd say to him the moment he reached out to hug her.

'You couldn't bring him back with you?'

'He's your brother, Miranda. How much ability do I have to influence him?'

'More than I do,' she retorted dryly. 'Charlotte is understandably pissed off. When's he going to get fitted for his suit?'

'These are good questions my love, but more importantly, did you read my *Crocodile catches crook* piece and watch the video?

'Crocodile! What have you boys been up to? Give me your phone now. I wanna see it.' Miranda read the article with alarm then amusement.

Crocodile catches crook

A drug smuggler got more than he bargained for when he attempted to transport sixty kilos of cocaine through the Cape Conway National Park. Ignoring warning signs throughout the park he lingered a little too long at the edge of a creek which is renowned as a popular place for female crocodiles to nurse their young. Sergeant Kirra Sillago reported that he was lucky to have only received a nip from a juvenile crocodile.

'So how did you manage to get the inside scoop on this story?' Miranda asked.

'I got to meet Sergeant Sillago and some of the other characters who helped to catch the drug smugglers while I was on Hamilton Island. A few, including your brother and your best friend, don't wish to reveal their involvement in the incident.'

'Scott and Charlotte? Why didn't they tell me about this?'

'Because we needed to wait until criminal charges had been laid, which they have now. You can read about it in my piece today's *Whitsunday Times*.'

How we caught 'The Tiger'

Pedro Gatos, also known as *The Tiger* and owner of the yachts *Ojo del Tigre* and *Latin Libertad*, was today incited on drug trafficking charges along with accomplices Juan Gomez, Scott *The Squrrel* Harmon, Fred Senen, Brian *Bluey* Black and Charley Chubb. Sergeant Kirra Sillago reported that the cartel had been covertly tracked by customs officials and the US Drug Enforcement Administration agency for over a year.

However it was a local man Nev Googaburra, who was key to securing the evidence that brought the cartel down. Nev, or *Nonsense* as he's affectionately known in the Whitsunday area, is a Ngaro elder and retired tracker who not only found the smugglers but was able to hide the sixty kilograms of cocaine until police arrived. Additionally, crucial photos were taken by investigative journalist Mason Murray in the Fish D'vine and The Rum Bar on Tuesday evening. No further comment was available from local police at this time.

'My god. Scott's been arrested! On drug trafficking charges!' Miranda shrieked.

'No no no no nooooooooo my love. That's another Scott Harmon, also known as *The Squirrel*.'

'Thank goodness for that. I'd better call Mum and Dad before they read this. They don't need any more stress with the wedding just over a week away.' Miranda took out her phone before adding, 'So if Scott's not in jail, where is he?'

SCOTT: FRI 12 FEB 8:00AM

Scott spoke to his father, explaining he was working a quick job, that he'd be back on the 19th, and that Charlotte was in charge of finding him a suit. He agreed it was a pity he was going to miss the get together on the 14th, and reassured his dad that he'd spend time with his grandparents at the wedding. With the call to his father ticked off his pre-departure check list, Scott called Charlotte. She was in a better frame of mind than the previous day but had clearly not forgiven him for taking another job so close to the wedding.

'I'm good thank you. Setting sail tonight. Yes, I've spoken to Mum. Yes, I'll work on my best man's speech en route. Yes. I'm missing you already...'

CHARLOTTE: VALENTINE'S DAY

There'd been ten text messages and two calls since he'd set sail for Brisbane. Charlotte had little time to remain angry as she was busy planning games and ordering gorgeous cupcakes and tiny sandwiches for the bridal shower/rehearsal dinner, which was now called the Friends, Family and Love celebration. She'd also chosen a bridesmaid dress and ordered Scott's suit. Tick. Tick.

Her parent's house at Kangaroo Point was crowded and ringing with laughter by 3:00pm on Valentine's Day. Charlotte wore a colourful outfit made with fabric she'd bought in Thailand. However, by the arrival of the third guest she wished she'd worn a t-shirt instead, emblazoned with *Scott is sailing and yes he'll be back for the wedding.*

Everyone enjoyed the high tea and the silly questions asked about Miranda and Mason through the pass-the-parcel game. Finally, everyone settled in a chair or on a pillow on the floor to watch the slide show. The lights went down and an opening image of Miranda and Charlotte in their nippers' outfits at Byron Bay Surf lifesaving club caused everyone to coo with delight. This was followed by a snap of them playing in the long grass at their grandparents' house at Bangalow. Miranda's early interest in Mason was obvious in the third image of her watching him apply sunscreen. There were photos of Miranda and Charlotte lying on the grass in the back yard, studying together, playing dress up and modelling Charlotte's many designs. There were several photos of Mason in London with his flatmates. Charlotte had included a photo of the bathroom in the flat in West Kensington, prompting everyone to say *Ooooh*. Next, the slide show jumped to France and there were pictures of Scott and Mason standing on the pier in Antibes and on a hill in Cannes. The photo of Mason in a dinner jacket at the Rose Ball in Monaco prompted comments about how handsome he was along with queries as to Charlotte's presence while he was at the ball.

'I had a modelling thing on,' Charlotte replied, not revealing that she was actually at the ball as a body double for Princess Charlotte. Finally, there was the image of a beaming Miranda and clearly pleased-with-himself Mason, clinking champagne glasses at the Vertigo sky-high restaurant in Bangkok the night they got engaged. A round of applause followed and the lights were turned on. More photos were taken and hugs distributed as guests collected their heart-shaped cupcakes and said goodbye.

'That was so wonderful C. Thank you,' Miranda said, giving her friend a tight hug.

'My pleasure M. See you at the hairdressers at 9:00 next Saturday.'

24

CHARLOTTE: FRI 19 FEB

Charlotte's diary entries

Noon. Scott just called to let me know he's only three hours away from entering the mouth of the Brisbane River. Flip he's cutting it fine. Delayed. Waiting on delivery of new sail.

6:00 pm Scott called to say the sail's operational but there's a large cruise ship at Hamilton broken down and restricting traffic. Groan. Wonder if I'm getting high blood pressure.

7:00pm Cancelled evening out with Miranda for hens' night as she's feeling anxious that Scott's not home yet. Spent two hours on phone providing counselling support.

10:00 pm Scott texted rather than called, (the coward), to say they've anchored for the night and will be sailing up the river at first light. Have been practicing breathing more slowly.

20 February, Miranda and Mason's Wedding Day

6:00am Yay. Sun is shining although forecast suggests possible late breaking thunderstorms for M&M's special day.

7:00am. Wrapped Scott's suit in tissue paper and packed it carefully in a suitcase ready to take it to the venue. Just in case.

8:00am Yay. Call from Scott to say he's back in Brisbane. Drove suit plus shoes over to the Murrays' house where the boys are getting changed.

9:00am Loving belated hens' party while at the Fox and Hair hairdresser with Miranda, her mum Jenny Harmon, her grandmother Helen Harmon, Mason's mum Lauren Murray, and my wonderful mum, Melissa Wyatt. So much joy between the women folk and a bit too much champagne from glasses trimmed with cascading pink fairy floss.

25

SCOTT: SAT 20 FEB 7:30AM

Mason's chattiness was delightful and nerve wracking in equal measure. But then I'd been on my own for the last week and had temporarily lost the art of conversation.

I'd arrived on the morning of the wedding, just as the Murray family were enjoying a last breakfast together with Mason as a bachelor. *Star Trek* jokes, embarrassing childhood stories and occasional tears were plentiful and I was pleased to be a contributor. Later, in Mason's old room, I opened the suitcase Charlotte had dropped off earlier, *I love that girl*, and grinned when I opened an envelope marked *see you soon*, containing my beaded-leather, lucky wrist band. I didn't call her as I knew she was in the bosom of female companionship at the hair-dressers but sent an emoji of a cockatoo instead. I knew she'd get it.

A silver limousine delivered us to the Kangaroo Point parklands at 11:00am and I was blown away by the beauty of the setting. The Kangaroo Point cliffs provided a dramatic rugged backdrop to the sparkling riverside, with sweeping views from the city skyline to the botanical gardens and up the Brisbane River. A dozen yachts were anchored a short distance from shore, and I was pleased to see my dinghy still firmly secured to a nearby pier. We hugged all the guests, twice, and then took our official spots at the front of the rows of white chairs facing the river, under a flower threaded pergola.

'She's here,' Helen Harmon called out, sending the signal for the pianist and cellist to start playing Pachelbel's Canon in D. We turned slowly to watch Miranda emerge between the gum trees, and seemingly glide up the centre passageway between the chairs. Mason took off his glasses and I passed him a handkerchief to wipe away the tears. My focus moved from my beautiful sister to Charlotte, who had been momentarily out of sight, behind the bride. She wore a spectacular silver sleeveless dress and carried a bunch of white roses. It was easy to see how she could pass as a princess and I resisted the urge to break from my best man role and wrap her in my arms. I stared at her unblinking, as Mason and Miranda exchanged vows. When the celebrant announced them man and wife, Miranda's Uncle Fred hit the play button on his phone and the guests rose to clap and jig along to Pharrel Williams' song, 'Happy'.

The wedding party then moved to a rocky outcrop for photos while the guests moved to a marquee fifty metres away to enjoy cocktails and canapés. I put his arm around Charlotte's waist while waiting for directions from the photographer. Nuzzling her neck, I whispered

'You look amazing, Princess Charlotte.'

With photos completed we all returned to take our seats in the marquee. After dinner, Uncle Fred announced the commencement of the speeches.

Scott's Best Man's Speech

This is such a perfect day. The joy I feel in seeing my best friend marry my sister is hard to describe. We've always been a part of each other's lives and this marriage not only joins two quirky, and wonderful, people together, but more strongly connects a community of families who love you both very much and are here to give you a send-off that will keep you warm, which is so important when you're freezing your butts off in Mason's flat. To Mason and Miranda.

Father of the Bride's Speech

Thank you Scott for that message. It's great to have you here and I can't convey how relieved your mother and I are that you weren't the Scott Harmon caught up with that nasty drug cartel on the Whitsundays.

There were snickers among the guests and Scott squeezed Charlotte's hand then lifted his wine glass to his father.

Such a special day and I'm such a proud father. Jenny and I could not be happier for you, Miranda. We welcome Mason with open arms and look forward to hearing all about your life in London together, and to visiting you at some stage. Take that as when you have your own place with a clean bathroom. Please don't stay away too long. We love you and we'll miss you terribly. Have a wonderful life. To Mason and Miranda.

Mason's Speech

Miranda. Marvellous Miranda. Thank you for marrying me and for agreeing to come to London to start our life together, which I know will initially be a little tricky sharing the flat with Kev, Will, Tom and Simon... (laughter from the guests).

And thank you everyone else for coming today to join our celebration. It's a wonderful feeling for Mrs Murray and I to be here in the company of so many people we love.

All the guests chinked their wine glass with their dessert spoons as if they were percussion instruments.

It's been such a fun journey to this point. Most of you know that Miranda and I first got to know each other as nippers at the Byron Bay Surf Club, and we'd bump into each other kinda frequently because we had best mates who knew each other. So we got to know each other slowly, and love just crept up on us.

Mason looked at Miranda and leant over to kiss her.

So enjoy the party everybody. And as Miranda and I embark on the next stage of our life together, we wish you the best with yours.

Mason looked at Scott with a curious expression while everyone clapped. The bride and groom walked out onto the dance floor as Uncle Fred reignited the playlist, blasting out Elton John's song, 'Can You Feel the Love Tonight'. Scott reached for Charlotte's hand and led her on to the dance floor as well.

'Good speech,' Charlotte offered, snuggling in close.

'Thank you. Dad's was good too, but only cause I got him to remove a couple of embarrassing stories about Miranda as a toddler.'

'Thanks for that. Miranda thanks you for that too. What are your plans now? Your last job's over, isn't it?'

'Indeed, it is. My plans are very clear. In ten minutes, I'm going to sequester you away on that dinghy over there.'

Charlotte laughed. 'We can't, Scott. It's rude to leave before the bride and groom.'

'I've spoken with them and they're fine with it, particularly as they're planning their own early departure. They've got to make the most of their honeymoon before Mason flies back to London.'

'Alright then. I'll scoot around and say goodbye to everyone and see you in five.'

Scott took her hand as Charlotte removed her high heeled shoes and stepped into the dinghy. It had been such a beautiful and perfect day. She looked back to the foreshore and saw Miranda and Mason watching them. They waved and she blew them back air kisses as they headed out into the middle of the river. She then noticed that their parents were also watching them from the rocky outcrop where the wedding photos had been taken. More energetic waving and air kisses followed.

'What do you think?' Scott asked pointing at the yacht in front of them.

'*Nonsense in the North?*' Charlotte said incredulously,

reading the name painted on the hull of the yacht. 'Whose yacht is this?'

'Used to be the *Latin Libertad*, owned by Pedro Gatos. But I got a tip off that it was being auctioned at a police station in Bundaberg.'

'Does that mean what I think it means?'

'Yes, it does. It's mine. And I'd like to make it ours. So, Charlotte Wyatt, would you be open to sailing off into the sunset with me for a life of nonsense?'

'Are you asking me what I think you're asking me?'

Scott smiled and leant forward to give her a long and tender kiss.

'Well, as long as it's just the two of us and you won't be picking up any cargo along the way.'

'Agreed,' Scott replied.

'But we shouldn't tell anyone. It's Miranda and Mason's big day,' Charlotte continued. Scott, busy hoisting the sails, didn't reply.

'Scott? Did you hear what I said?' A sudden gust of wind filled the sails, and there followed shouting, whistling and clapping from the wedding guests now sprinkled along the river's edge.

'What's going on?' she asked. He pointed to the mainsail where the words 'She said YES' were written in an enormous font. Charlotte started laughing as fireworks exploded from a nearby barge, an event arranged secretly by Mason and Scott. It was a spectacular end to the day. As they sailed down the Brisbane River, Scott at the wheel, Charlotte hugged him from behind and asked, 'What are your plans for the yacht? Are you going to charter it out, I mean, how are we going to make money?'

'Well, now you ask, I've had a bit of an interesting job offer from Teal Dubois.'

EPILOGUE

One month later

Charlotte called her parents from Hook Island to tell them to keep 5 September free for a wedding.

Scott texted Teal to decline the *interesting* job offer.

Miranda found a job in London. She and Mason were able to move out of the shared West Kensington flat into a place of their own.

Mason accepted a new position at *The Independent* newspaper, leaving the world of high fashion behind.

Pedro Gatos and Juan Gomez both received twenty-five-year jail sentences for unlawfully trafficking a Schedule 1 drug. Fred, Bluey and *the chubby one* received ten-year sentences for unlawfully trafficking a Schedule 1 drug. Scott Harmon number two, also known as *The Squirrel*, received a five-year sentence for money laundering.

Bill Cowboy resigned as local member for Nirvana due to ill health.

Yindi was inundated with orders for her unique Aboriginal fabrics in the week following Mason's pictorial in *Hello*.

Kirra was promoted to lieutenant.

Nonsense continued fishing and remained on call as an occasional tracker for his favourite lieutenant.

THANKS FOR READING

I hope you enjoyed reading *Nonsense in the North*. I had tonnes of fun writing this last book in the Northern Rivers Series in my native Australia.

I'd love to know what you thought of the story if you have the time to pen me a few lines. I get a kick out of chatting with readers.

Below are my contact details and social media hangouts.

- Email me at janeellyson@gmail.com and I'm also on
- Twitter @janeellyson1– if you're a tweeter, on Facebook https://www.facebook.com/jane.ellyson.7 and Pinterest
- https://www.pinterest.com.au/janeellyson/pins/and Instagram
- https://www.instagram.com/janeellyson/ on Goodreads

- https://www.goodreads.com/author/show/ 17708285.Jane_Ellyson

If you enjoyed the story, please tell your friends and write a review online. You can do this on Goodreads (link above) or wherever you bought the book.

I share insights into how I wrote each of the stories in the Northern River Series through my monthly newsletter. You can sign up at www.janeellyson.com

I've provided the prequel to Over Byron Bay, called Boy from Bangalow. It's where the series started and was written because of reader feedback that they wanted to know more about Andrew Wyatt and Melissa Bourne's relationship at university.

Happy reading,

Best
    Jane

BOY FROM BANGALOW (PREQUEL TO OVER BYRON BAY)

BOY
FROM
BANGALOW
Prequel to
Over
Byron Bay
Jane Ellyson

Map: Ballina to Brisbane

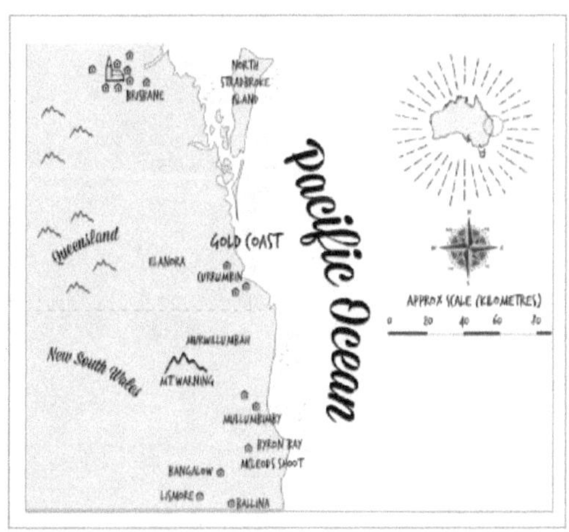

I. CONVERSATION IN THE CAFE

'A penny for your thoughts'. Startled, Melissa glanced up to see the familiar face of a neighbour.

'Ah the boy from Brisbane is back.'

'You mock me. I'll always be the boy from Bangalow.' She smiled.

'Haven't you taken up rowing and decided to study law? Both decisions influenced by that posh boarding school in Brisbane?'

'Both pursuits will enable me to live a comfortable life. I'll get to spend time on the water, (which I love),' he declared with emphasis, 'right the wrongs of the world and one day drive a Beemer.'

'I see.'

'And you? What are you studying?'

'Art and design.'

'Ah that's the reason for this,' he said tapping the book of landscapes open in front of her while sitting down uninvited on the small bench. He squeezed close to her as and she regarded him carefully. He smelt of freshly laundered washing. She looked into his smiling eyes, a little unnerved.

'No, not really. This book is for another purpose. I'm creating a ruse to get Dad out of the house.'

'Ahh. How is he. It's been what, well over a year since your Mum passed?'

'Yeah. Eighteen months now and Dad's still a hermit. He rarely goes out and he won't let me give away Mum's clothes that are still hanging in their wardrobe. Conversations are limited to me and *Boy*. That dog is such a lifeline but Dad needs other adult, human company. His friends from the Uni have stopped calling so I thought I'd get him to come here to Lismore, which is why I signed up for this.' Melissa slipped a pamphlet across the table announcing The Great Debate between the faculties. I've been telling him I need support so he has to come.'

'I see. Cunning plan.'

'You coming?' she enquired.

'Indeed I am. I'll be sharing the stage with you, arguing the case that *the pen is indeed mightier than the paint brush*.' Melissa looked up at the ceiling, closed her eyes and gently shook her head.

'I should've guessed. Any opportunity to argue.' He smiled revealing a set of slightly crooked, pearly white teeth. 'Will your parents be coming?'

'They might do, particularly now that they know who I'm up against.'

'Would be nice to catch up with your Mum'.

'There you are,' came a sultry voice from the entrance to the café. A short-haired siren, sashayed across the room and sat down on Andrew's lap, a clear sign of ownership.

'Melissa, this is Simone.' That would be *Simone Number Seven* Melissa calculated.

'Hi Simone,' she offered in a deadpan voice while looking at Andrew.

'Come Andy. Let's go.' Simone stood and looked expectantly at him.

'Ok then.' He said as a sigh. 'All the best with your preparation.' Melissa nodded, her head ever so gently, acknowledging him.

'See you at the debate *Andy*', Melissa offered, biting her lip to hide a smirk.

'Good luck with getting your Dad to come. I'll ask Mum to drop off a few nectarines and have a bit of a natter. She's pretty good at cajoling people.'

'Ta. That'd be appreciated.' Simone tugged on his sleeve, he stood and put his arm loosely around her waist. Melissa watched them walk to the door. Andrew threw her a glance before following Simone down the steps. She turned another page in her book but looked up distractedly, thinking about Andrew's latest girlfriend. She mentally noted the names of the other women Andrew has courted. There was *Angst ridden Anne, Mia the Model, Bookish Belinda* and *Inky Ingrid*, whose neck tatts made her more than a little scary. She'd not met either Zoe or Kalinda, who Andrew's mother described as well-mannered. (She was sure she was holding back on what she really thought if this was all she could say.)

Andrew's mother Emily had been a wonderful support for her when her mother was dying, often calling by with something fresh from Byron markets. And she always had time for a cuppa, when she needed somewhere calm away from the house. Melissa didn't have to talk, which was good because she didn't want to. It was somewhere safe to sit while Emily chatted about what her four sons were up to. Andrew had joined a friend at boarding school in Brisbane, which was 170 kilometres away, so Melissa only saw him intermittently during the previous two years. With their families owning adjoining farms, she more frequently saw his brothers tending cattle. Her eyes returned to her book, her mother's book, which included sketches and paintings from her mother's home state of Maine. They'd been planning a family trip before her mother was diagnosed with cancer. At that moment she missed her mother terribly and tears filled her eyes. She discreetly wiped them away and returned to debate preparation.

II. THE GREAT DEBATE

It was raucous in Lecture room 4 on Friday evening. New graduates were decked out in costumes from the 19th century, playing out roles of prominent politicians, lawyers and artists. The great debate was the penultimate event in orientation week, so everyone was in high spirits. Melissa's eye's flickered to her father. He was supressing a smile. He was back in familiar territory. He had finally taken the shirt she gave him for Christmas out of the wrapper and he looked good.

'George,' came a voice from the front row. It was Marty Gordon, a fellow lecturer from the science faculty.

'It's fairly clear which case you'll be supporting tonight.'

'No Marty, as always, I'll be objective and guided by the facts as presented.' His friend chortled.

'Good to see you George, and to know you've not lost your sense of humour.' He took the last seat on the end of the fifth row, still keeping a little distance from others.

The familiar *tat tat tat* of fingernails on the microphone preceded a wave of hushes across the room.

Everyone took their seat and turned their attention to the master of ceremonies, formally attired in her graduation gown and cap. Octavia Hildengard was a formidable woman. She was one of the first women to become Vice-Chancellor in Australia. Her intellect and wit were well known.

'Good evening and welcome. Wonderful to see all the costumes tonight. I appreciated the conversation with academic and former president of the United States Woodrow Wilson, on income tax policy and racial segregation.'

'Oh,' is whispered across the room.

'And it was lovely to chat with English painter Helen Allingham on how she chose her wonderful landscape subjects. Tonight's topic is a cheeky play on the well-known adage that *the pen is mightier than the sword*. Here at Southern Cross University, we leave the study of military strategy to our colleagues at the Royal Military College in Duntroon, Canberra, choosing to focus instead in many other areas including the arts and law. So, tonight we will hear arguments for and against the proposition that *the pen is mightier than the paintbrush.*

It's my pleasure to introduce the debaters whose arguments may challenge your thinking or entertain you. I've asked both speakers to provide me with personal insights that many others wouldn't know. Arguing for the affirmative is Andrew Wyatt. Andrew is a first-year student in the faculty of law. His ambition is to ensure fairness and equity for everyone. In terms of something personal, Andrew's family produces the best mangoes in Bangalow.'

'Onya Andrew,' comes a cry from a fellow student and Simone stands, enthusiastically clapping, prompting everyone else to join. When the clapping fades the Chair continued.

'Melissa is a first-year student in the faculty of art and design. Her ambition is to travel widely and use design to bring beauty to the everyday. Something personal about Melissa, her father produces the best lychees in the Northern Rivers Region.' Everybody laughed and some of the academic staff started cheering. George Bourne beamed. A wide grin erupted across Melissa's face. This evening has already delivered the value she'd hoped for. Now to get this darn debate done.

The Chair nodded to Andrew to take his position behind the lectern in the centre of the stage. He momentarily shuffled the papers, took a deep breath, looked up at the audience, paused for a moment, and then smiled. He has their undivided attention.

Madam Chair, students and guests.

In my hand I hold a source of great power.

(Andrew holds up a pen)

This humble instrument can explain rights and obligations, creating a safer and fairer world for all. The written word can encourage civilised behaviour, facilitate consensus in disputes, and inspire political action.

Laws reflect the values of the society within which they exist, and with the power of the pen, these laws can evolve to echo changing values and aspirations.

These values reflect how power is organised, exercised and controlled. At their heart, our laws reject unfairness, support dignity and mercy and insist on equality for all.

These are just some of the reasons why the pen has such an influence on our society and why I am proud to advocate that the pen is mightier than the paintbrush.

But pens do more than write laws.

They can also explain philosophy often written down in books such as The Bible, Plato's Republic, Marx's Das Kapital and Darwin's Origin of Species. Think of a book that has influenced you by the inspiration of the vision or the power of the argument.

With a pen we can also write love letters.

(Andrew pauses and a murmur erupts among the female members of the audience.)

For example, from Prince Albert to Queen Victoria. *(Andrew reads dramatically)*

Dearest deeply loved Victoria, I need not tell you that since we left, all my thoughts have been with you at Windsor, and that your image fills my whole soul. Even in my dreams I never imagined that I should find so much love on earth.

Or from Orson Welles to Rita Hayworth *(Andrew reads slowly and gently)*

... I suppose most of us are lonely in this big world, but we must fall tremendously in love...to find it out.

(Melissa looks at her father who is affected by the words.)

And finally, a love sonnet from Elizabeth Barrett Browning.

How do I love thee? Let me count the ways.

I love thee to the depth and breadth and height my soul can reach

If this last line does not convince you of the power of words transcribed by the pen *(Andrew held the pen up),*

I'm not sure what will.

Thank you.

Andrew returns to his chair to rapturous applause led by chants of Andy, Andy, Andy from Simone, and several other girls who are snapping photos on their phones. He looked across to Melissa and winks, infuriating her. When the clapping subsides, she walks purposefully to the lectern, grasped its edges, and held a power pose. She scanned the room, took a deep breath and counted to three.

Madam Chair, lovers of learning, lovers of life, *(she paused)* lovers of love.

It's true. A pen allows us to communicate, but only to communicate in one way, through the written language of the author. We're lucky that here in this auditorium we speak the common language of English which is the third most popular spoken language in the world behind Mandarin at number one and Spanish at number two.

Did you know that there are 4,000 written languages and over 6,500 spoken languages in the world? A single language is useful when the one community speaks in the same voice – but when we take a broader view, a global view, what channel has a universal capacity to communicate meaning and emotion beyond the written word?

(She paused again for effect)

I propose that it is the paintbrush or indeed any form of the arts that provides a universal language, and that it's been this way since the very beginning.

Think of the way indigenous communities here in Australia have shared their history over time. They've used oral storytelling and song as well as visual communication through drawing and painting. With no written language, many depended for their very survival on maps of country with painted landmarks to remember where food and water could be located.

My learned colleague Mr Wyatt seems very interested in using the pen for the making of rules and the creation of order. He shared wonderful aspirations for what we want the law to achieve, but some laws from the past and even those in the present, have subjugated people. He shared moving passages of love and there are those in the room who've formalised their love in a marriage contract which of course was originally created to ensure that women would remain dependent and subservient after marriage. Many of course have gained the power to own and control property, to vote and to choose the direction of their lives. I think of wonderful American 19th century impressionist painter Mary Cassatt, who is represented in the room this evening.

(A girl in the first row, who is delighted at having been recognised, stood and curtsied to Melissa, pivoted, curtsied to the audience, and then retook her seat. Not missing a beat, Melissa continued.)

Apart from being a wonderful painter, Mary Cassatt was also a feminist who recognised that marriage would be detrimental to her career and that women should *be someone* and not *something*.

You know, for me, life *as a creative* is not so much about making the rules but about breaking them; of challenging the status quo to achieve those things that Mr Wyatt mentioned like fairness, equity and justice; but also to feel joy, to experience beauty and to come to understand the very nature of the human condition. This is what art gives us and this is *why the paintbrush is more powerful than the pen.*

The audience is stunned. Melissa confidently nodded at the Vice Chancellor and resumed her seat. An enthusiastic round of applause rose from the auditorium. Andrew clapped rigorously as well, and looked at her as he stood and walked across the stage, and again took his place behind the lectern.

My word Miss Bourne, I feel your passion. Don't you? *(He addressed to the audience)*

This is the first time I've been introduced to your revolutionary inclinations. Bravo.

I feel I need to respond to your concerning comments about the contract of marriage. Marriage has evolved. It's true that historically in most cultures, married women had very few rights of their own, being considered, along with the family's children, the property of the husband; as such, they could not own or inherit property, or represent themselves. However, since the late 19th century, marriage has undergone gradual legal changes, aimed at improving the rights of the wife and the children of the marriage. It's now an institution in many but not all parts of the world, entered into freely with obligations and protections shared and with objectives for companionship, personal growth and love. We have not reached utopia and like all aspects of the law, it needs to be reviewed, tested and updated.

You know, I think of other revolutionaries like Alexander Hamilton who also studied law. He was a man born out of wedlock, orphaned as a child who grew up to become an American statesman, politician, legal scholar, military commander, lawyer, banker, economist and one of the Founding Fathers of the United States, who was active in ending the legality of the international slave trade. He demonstrated the power of the pen to bring positive change, enriching the lives of others.

Miss Bourne, your points about art being a universal language are well made. However, I urge caution. Paintings can be ambiguous, which is dangerous when clarity is needed. The meaning to one person may not be the same as the meaning to another, and in a world where we want fairness and equity, we cannot afford the uncertainty that comes from ambiguity.

In closing, the law affects every part of our lives and the pen that writes our laws provides certainty and a foundation for a civil society. A pen can also be the vehicle for the distillation of philosophy and for the communication of love.

(Andrew paused).

And for these reasons I strongly submit that the pen is indeed mightier than the paintbrush.

A raucous round of applause fills the great hall. Andrew returned to his seat and Melissa moved quickly to the podium. She waited for a moment for the noise to subside.

The time for speaking is over. I need to let the power of art *(she paused)* speak for itself.

(The house lights dimmed and a 1964 painting by Norman Rockwell appears on the projector. Melissa stood and looked at the images for ten seconds before returning to the audience).

It's moving isn't it? You may not know the back story but you can feel the fear and feel the prejudice.

This 1964 painting by Norman Rockwell of Ruby Bridges is considered an iconic image from the Civil Rights Movement in the United States. Ruby was just a six-year-old African American girl, on her way to School, an all-white public school, during the New Orleans' school desegregation crisis of 1960. Because of threats of violence against her, she was escorted by four deputy U.S. marshals. On the wall behind her, you can see written the racial slur "nigger" and the impact of a splattered tomato thrown against the wall.

And another example.

(Melissa clicked on the next slide. A post-impressionist painting from the 19th century called Fields of Roussilion by Renee Gandy is displayed).

(Melissa again paused giving the audience time to examine the image.)

It's beautiful, isn't it? You may not have been there but you can already smell the lavender.

A painting can be a thing of beauty, inspiring us to pick up a paintbrush or to get out of our chair and to travel the world. To see things not seen before, to experience new tastes, breathe in new scents and explore new feelings. And speaking of feelings …

(Melissa clicked on the final image of a painting by Carolus-Duran – le Baiser)

(Melissa paused. There were ah from the audience.)

Can you feel the love tonight? Isn't this a wonderful image? Made even more special by the knowledge that this is a self-portrait of French painter Carolus Duran – le Baiser with his wife as newlyweds from 1868.

So, you can put your pens away. No words are needed here. Indeed, the paintbrush provides a universal language for all. It can mount an argument without words. Communicate beauty, reveal complexity, and allow us to experience love.

The act of painting, not only helps to develop our critical thinking but enables us to interpret the world around us.

And importantly, art brings us joy. And for these reasons (she paused) the power of the paintbrush surpasses the power of the pen.

(House lights return).

'Bravo.' George Bourne cried out, already on his feet clapping. He's soon joined by Andrew's parents and many others in the surrounding rows. Melissa smiled and returned to her seat. Octavia Hildengard was clapping as well with a huge grin across her face.

'My word. I don't know about you, but I'm quivering. I do not envy the task in front of our judges. What wonderful orators. Please join with me in thanking again our debaters.' There are cheers from the audience with Simone and a few friends attempting unsuccessfully to start a Mexican wave across the room. 'While our judges confer, it's my pleasure to announce the runners up and winner of the best costume from the 19th century.' She opened an envelope. 'The second runner-up is Michelle Kwee for her Daisy Bates costume. Please come up here Michelle to collect your prize. For those of you not familiar with this 19th century figure, Daisy Bates was an Australian journalist, welfare worker and lifelong student of Australian aboriginal culture.'

Photos were taken and the Vice Chancellor returned to the microphone.

'The first runner-up prize goes to Harry Leavon for his inspired interpretation of the Australian writer and bush poet, Henry Lawson. Come up here Harry. I wonder if you chose Henry Lawson because of the similarity of your names or because you wanted to try out that outrageous moustache?' Harry grinned, wiggled his moustache, and shook the Chairs hand, before taking his envelope, smiling for the photographer, and returning to his seat. 'And the winner of the best costume goes to Elizabeth Fleur for her portrayal of

Dame Nellie Melba who was ...' At this point an operatic voice can be heard singing, *There's no place like home,* from the back of the room. A polite round of applause ripples across the room and the chatter fell silent while people listened to the singer. 'Please join with me in congratulating our winner Dame Nellie Melba, also known as Elizabeth Fleur.' A small girl with strong lungs, dark, tight curls squeezed under a tiny bonnet and wearing a long-sleeved dress with satin pinafore, climbs the steps to the stage to collect her envelope and to pose for photos with the Vice-Chancellor. More applause followed.

'Well everyone. I've just been given the judges verdict. I invite Andrew Wyatt and Melissa Bourne to come stand with me. I think you'd all agree that they have represented their respective faculties brilliantly this evening.' One of the judges walked on to the stage with two wrapped boxes, one much larger than the other. 'In announcing the runner-up, I know that I will be simultaneously announcing the winner. In reality there is very little distance between the two. So, without further ado, I declare the runner up in our Orientation Great Debate on the topic that *the pen is mightier than the paintbrush* is Andrew Wyatt. Andrew beams as though he has been announced the winner.

'Thank you everybody. That concludes the formal part of the evening.' A photographer signalled for Andrew and Melissa to join the Vice-Chancellor for a photo in front of the university coat of arms.

'Are your parents nearby?' the photographer asks. They both nodded and waved their parents over for a photo.

'Well done Mel,' Charles Wyatt offered before patting his son on the back.

'You were brilliant,' Emily Wyatt whispered to Melissa, 'and you weren't too bad either son,' kissing him on the cheek. George Bourne beamed and took his place in the line-up for the photo. Several snaps later, the photographer asked for photos just with the winner and runner-up.

'I want you to strike a defensive pose.' Melissa and Andrew pass their presents to their parents, who look on curiously. They stood close to each other and struck a position as though they are boxing. Andrew didn't blink as he looked into her eyes. She felt unnerved and was aware that her heart had started beating faster. 'And now I want a photo as though you have just made up.' Melissa proactively put her hand out, offering to shake his hand. He smiled accepting her hand and stepped closer towards her. The camera starts clicking. When the photographer put the camera back into their bag, Andrew held on to Melissa's hand.

'I don't think that you'll be using your gift very much.'

'Au contraire. For a lawyer in training, you make a lot of assumptions. Certainly, this is a writing instrument with which I can write down my dreams and my thoughts, and my aspirations and my fears. But you only see it in one way. It's also a thing of beauty. Look at the colour. Look at the lines. Look at the beautiful gold tip. This is a piece of art that will bring pleasure to my life, simply by being. It's also a relic and a connection to a time that's passed. I'll take pleasure from it in a number of ways. Unlike those paint brushes of yours that are unlikely to get wet any time soon.' Andrew raises his eyebrows.

'Now, who's making assumptions?' Melissa looks into his lovely smiling eyes again.

'Touché.'

'You done?' Simone called out to Andrew from across the room.

'He's all yours,' Melissa returns.

'See you round.' Andrew touched her softly on the elbow and then saunters across the room to join Simone.

'Ready oh slayer of the legal profession.'

She kissed her father on the cheek and looped her arm through his.

'You bet.'

III. NEW PERSPECTIVES

Melissa wakes the following morning to an unfamiliar noise. It's not the cows mooing in the home paddock, or the kookaburras laughing from the back fence. It's the wonderful sound of her father rustling about in the kitchen. He's out of bed early for the first time in months. Grabbing her dressing gown and slipping on her Ugg boots, she joins him.

'Tea's in the pot,' he says in the most wonderful, normal voice as though they had shared this ritual every day. 'And we're out of lychees. Can you go pull a few for brekkie?'

'Of course, Dad.' She swapped her sheepskin slippers for her RM Williams boots, picked up a small bucket and headed down the garden path to the row of lychee trees. As she pulled a dozen of the deep crimson fruit from the branches, her eyes detect movement three paddocks away. She smiled when she spotted the familiar red flannel shirt and returned inside, placing the bucket on the kitchen bench.

'I'll get something to eat later Dad,' she called out as

she headed to her bedroom to change. It's such a lovely day she reflected as she crossed the small bridge over Byron Creek. Two magpies were showing their offspring how to spread their wings in preparation for flight while three wallabies watched her carefully from their vantage point in the long grass. As she climbed the last fence separating the families' properties, she started laughing. Andrew looked up.

'So, you're coming to mock me again?'

'I did not mock you. I simply challenged your argument. Do not confuse the object with the subject.'

'I see you are keen to apply your new skills. Very commendable.'

'Will you be joining me? I have a spare paint canvas.'

'Not today,' she replied reaching into her backpack to pull out a notebook and her new pen. 'I need a different perspective today.'

'You probably also need sustenance. There's a coffee thermos, mugs, fresh bread and homemade mango jam in the picnic basket.

'Expecting me?' she asks softly.

Melissa's father watches them from the kitchen window and smiles. Turning to his dog he says,

'Come Boy. You can supervise me clearing out the wardrobe.'

REFERENCES

Elizabeth Barrett Browning

- https://poets.org/poem/how-do-i-love-thee-sonnet-43

History of legal contract for marriage

- Browning, E. B. (2013). Sonnets from the Portuguese. Doubleday.
- Salmon, M. (2016). *Women and the law of property in early America*. UNC Press Books.
- https://www.fedcourt.gov.au/
- https://www.countryliving.com/life/inspirational-stories/g4061/famous-love-letters/
- https://japingkaaboriginalart.com/articles/facts-about-aboriginal-art/
- https://www.babbel.com/en/magazine/the-10-most-spoken-languages-in-the-world#:~:text=Chinese%20%E2%80%94%201.3%20Billion%

20Native%20Speakers,spoken%20language%
20in%20the%20world.

About studying law

- https://www.trin.cam.ac.uk/undergraduate/
courses/law/why-study-law/
- https://en.wikipedia.org/
wiki/The_Problem_We_All_Live_With

ABOUT JANE ELLYSON

Jane has a deep connection to the Far North Coast of New South Wales where *Over Byron Bay* is set. Her great grandparents owned a farm a little way out of Byron Bay and her grandparents were long term residents of Mullumbimby. She currently lives at Possum Creek, not far out of Bangalow – well she would if she was real – rather than being the pen name of someone who would prefer to remain anonymous. This is her fifth and final novel in the Northern Rivers series.

www.janeellyson.com

janeellyson@gmail.com

OTHER BOOKS IN THE NORTHERN RIVERS SERIES

OVER
BYRON BAY
POOR TIMING AND AGONIES OF
CONSCIENCE ARE EVER PRESENT IN THIS
SWEET LOVE STORY
JANE ELLYSON
BOOK 1 OF 5

Over Byron Bay (Book 1 of 5)

Melissa Bourne and Andrew Wyatt were neighbours in the country town of Bangalow in Australia. Friends, good friends were all they'd ever been. This situation suited them both until Andrew found someone else. Surprised at her jealousy and with an international job offer in hand, Melissa left the country. She accepted a job offer in Boston, met Jonathan Brinkley, married and settled into life in the U.S.

Five years later she returns to Bangalow for a visit with her father, shortly after the death of Andrew's mother. The two meet briefly at the funeral, and the day before she flies back to Boston providing an opportunity to rekindle their relationship and to recognise that their feelings for each other go beyond friendship. Melissa returns to the States in turmoil.

SUBSTITUTE
CHILD

DISCOVERY OF A BOTTLE PROMPTS A
WHIRLWIND JOURNEY OF ADVENTURE, LOVE
AND A SEARCH FOR IDENTITY
JANE ELLYSON
BOOK 2 OF 5

Substitute Child (Book 2 of 5)

A deckhand in France discovers a bottle with a letter inside. The bottle has floated all the way from Byron Bay in Australia to the south of France. The discovery prompts a whirlwind journey for Charlotte Wyatt into the world of paparazzi, European royalty and the criminal underworld.

Substitute Child is the story of a student travelling to the other side of the world to collect a bottle with a love letter to a brother she never knew and a journey to discover who she is and what she wants from her life.

WHERE'S JACK?
ROMAN ROULETTE
MISSING FRIENDS AND THE MAFIA CAUSE
MAYHEM IN THE MEDITERRANEAN
JANE ELLYSON
BOOK 3 OF 5

Roman Roulette (Book 3 of 5)

Unable to leave Rome due to an air traffic controller strike, Charlotte accepts an invitation to a party on a super yacht. A friend disappears and then Charlotte becomes an accidental stowaway as the yacht heads for Sicily. Inadvertently caught up in the international slavery trade and forced to choose between several unbearable options, Charlotte embarks on a bold plan to save the women captured by the Monk, and in doing so, to save herself. Adventure/Thriller set between Rome, Naples and Taormina in Sicily.

MISSING
IN
MYANMAR
A SIMPLE REQUEST.
A JOURNEY TO A FOREIGN COUNTRY.
ALL BEFORE THE LIGHTS WENT OUT.
JANE ELLYSON
BOOK 4 OF 5

Missing in Myanmar (Book 4 of 5)

Charlotte Wyatt wasn't sure what she was letting herself in for when she agreed to be available for occasional information gathering activities for the Australian Securities Intelligence Organisation. Her first assignment comes at the end of a holiday in Thailand. Having just said goodbye to her boyfriend, who has taken a job sailing from Port Vila in Vanuatu to Bundaberg in Australia, Charlotte Wyatt is intrigued by the opportunity to go to Myanmar to gather information about a missing person.

With the help of a mysterious librarian, she finds the information she was sent to retrieve, and then, just as she's making plans to return, the lights go out in Myanmar and the military takes over. With a reluctant passenger, Charlotte runs checkpoints and dodges bullets, in a race to the border.

www.janeellyson.com

www.ingramcontent.com/pod-product-compliance
Lightning Source LLC
Chambersburg PA
CBHW030433120726
47903CB00003B/935